THE CC
IN WOMAN
AND OTHER TALES

DIANE KING

Beaten Track
www.beatentrackpublishing.com

The Colour in Woman and Other Tales

Published 2021 by Beaten Track Publishing
The Colour in Woman first published 2016
Copyright © 2016, 2021 Diane King

Paperback ISBN: 978 1 78645 498 0
eBook ISBN: 978 1 78645 499 7

Cover Design: Amanda Kelsey, Razzle Dazzle Design
Illustrations: Maryna Yakovchuk

Beaten Track Publishing,
Burscough, Lancashire.
www.beatentrackpublishing.com

CONTENTS

The
Colour
in
Woman

Dedicated to Margot, who would have read this
in the garden while listening to the birds.
Now reading it from the realms beyond.
This one is better than my psychology essays, Margot!

LEGACY

ONE

adore these still days. They carry the sweetness of late summer and the misty beckoning of autumn. It's a day like so many I have passed here while it was just my father and me. Although I can't remember if my mother had gone then or not, I do remember so many afternoons were passed in the garden, Dad putting a name to the screeches and cries cutting through the still, heavy air.

My garden is beautiful and huge. I woke up one morning and here it all was. When it is bright and searing, I will roam it all day, letting the rays from the hot sun slide over my body like butter, melting into my warm skin, making it glisten and smell salty-sweet. The smell, particularly if I lie on my front, chin on arms, reminds me of foreign holidays. That smell of sun cream, sweat, sand and that evasive foreign aroma always detectable abroad. The personal smell which has seeped out of your skin for a lifetime suddenly changes fragrance—not unpleasant, not pleasant. Just different. Then, when you get off the plane on your return home, your old faithful smell returns and clings to you. Except in hot summers when you sit in the garden.

Which is mostly what I do now I'm on my own. It's one of the quickest ways to go back, for it's the place where the past sits. Something from my childhood hangs in the air molecules. It must be those scents of sun cream and grass and hot skin.

The house I live in stands on the sweeping moorland. A fragmented woodland spurts at the base of the hills. When the weather is fine, chirpings and warbles resound through latticed twigs feathered with green and lilac. Blossoms litter the grass like angel lipstick blots, and fragrances make my nose buzz. But most of the time, a lot of the time, it is wild with rain and mist and wind and black tangles, black shadows, black trees.

There's a feeling I should...do...something. I'm not quite sure what it is, so I sit in the garden to see if it will come to me. I've a feeling I've forgotten something, but it's so close— that feeling when you go to say something and you forget and it's on the tip of your tongue. Yes, kind of like that. And when it's sunny, I feel like the secret, the answer, is in the massive garden I used to get lost in when I was a kid.

So then, I'll stay out in the garden.

I love to feel my hair in the sun—how it can be hot or cold. If my hair is hot, I press it to my head and wrap it around my face to drink in the warmth, absorb it deep into my blood and feel it fizz through my insides. If, on the other hand, it's cold, I push my hands into it from the base up and separate my fingers so a cool clump of hair spurts out between each one. I feel the freshness, the airiness breezing through, then slowly pull my fingers back down, pressing the cold hair to my skull, and feel the goosebumps ride over my body.

It is as though Dad is still with me. He's here somewhere in the garden, I'm sure. I can't really think or remember how this all became mine. He's here somehow. And yet, one day, I woke up and it was all mine!

And the house is alive. I scare myself in the night by waking from a nightmare, then creeping through the passages. Rugs scuff and crumple under my bare, hard feet, dark-red rugs with thick tassels and faded designs of yellow and cobalt that slide around on the old floor like synthetic snakes. I'll stand on the top landing then look down to the bottom floor, waiting for a glassy face to slide through the slats of the banisters. I'm always waiting. And then I forget what I'm waiting for as I gaze around my home, see the open window framing a moon-milky expanse, the pictures of animals on the walls like blocks of black-and-white wood, a toad with sparkling eyes squatting on a purple rock, the giant vases and candles, the beautiful green furniture in the library...

How did I get to have a library? I'm sure there's something in there I'm looking for, but there's so much to look at, I can't think of it.

I sometimes sleep in the library; I like the warmth. I keep all the curtains open to admire the outside—something I wasn't allowed to do when I was little. Maybe there was a fear I'd spot the fae and run away to them. Ha! At the bottom of the garden! And beyond...

There is a sigh breathing over this expanse past the bottom of the garden. The breath moves swiftly over the brown turf, the wild purple. It does not catch on the rocks or a solitary bush but caresses the texture and moulds the rough presence into the same harmony as the flowing land. There is no time. Now there is constancy.

The best time is early evening in the summer. The light dips and covers everything with a still softness, a moment of aged wisdom, a moment where secrets may be revealed. Birds circle in low flight, cutting through the syrupy air, their song catching in the sweet gloop. The thickness of the twilight is diluted by the lap and glisten of the distant lake, which sits and seems to...watch. It's been watching for a long time, I guess, which is kind of strange now I know what I do.

Secrets—they're everywhere! The universe itself hangs in the air, filters through the lake, the trees, the globules of water trembling on the tips of branches. Notice how they can tell you about simplicities of friendship and complexities of nature. These small globules of translucence will whisper how to live, will dance their way into your mind and saturate heavy limbs with their light knowledge, their pure knowledge, so fragile yet stronger than any building, as they balance so cleverly unaided. The secrets of the water bulbs tell you of the friendship. If you let them.

Raining, raining, raining, raining, raining, raining...over and over and over, and on and on, on, on, on, on, on...look at the droplets, look at the branches, shiny black strands holding the tiniest lights at the tips, quivering bulbs of water glisten from heaven, hypnotise...if you let them...

On the gate to my garden, there is a notice: No Trade Callers. I keep where the colours are raw and bright—let that lot hide beneath a sticky snail shell of grey and mud brown, trudging along their slimy path. It's not for me. When I was left, I gathered the colours to my chest and started to make them my own.

TWO

omewhere beyond the lake—beyond the lake and below the rough hills—there sat a small town. A town with cobbles and houses and thin streets and cats. And somewhere up a road and in a house and up some stairs lived a woman. A woman who lived alone. And yet not quite alone.

In the beginning were thoughts. Curiosity. The desire to find something else—anything else—and lose the other. The other her, suspended in that sacrificial point in time. It was all rather an interesting experiment. Who knew what might crop up?

So the woman started to drink. She'd enjoyed a bubbly or few back in the other days, when she'd been free in the evening or at a function. But now, she had the space of lions! No time restriction, no responsibilities, no duties. So she drank and read books and drank until the words fizzed off the page and into the room, popping in front of her. She would try to touch them, fit them into her pocket, put them in the kettle for boiling or see if she could eat them. They tantalised her with their evasive movement and she laughed. At least they would play with her. She'd managed to find something in this new life of hers.

As time passed, she drew her emerald chenille curtains and saturated her room with a porraceous hue and her body with red units. And she watched the words and laughed at their prettiness.

*

The first really curious thing to crop up was another woman who took form in the corner of her room. She appeared at intervals, and after every appearance came news of a death. And while waiting for further fascinating things to unfold, the drinking woman saturated her body with red and her room with green and read books in the air.

She discovered the woman who appeared in the corner of her room was a banshee. The floating words told her so. The banshee appeared from time to time and would sit with long, white hair and dress and stare into space. And the drinking woman would gaze at the banshee, rather like a lab sample in this experiment of hers, and wait for news of a death.

*

One day, the banshee appeared in the early morning. She sat and stared into space, and the woman waited. The banshee lingered and watched and did not vanish. This was an unexpected turn in the sampling. Interesting, but unexpected. After a period of time, the woman read her floating words and found an old suggestion for encounters with forms of this kind. The old wives said there are particular words to be spoken, and so the woman turned to the white apparition in the corner of her room, who had been there for eight days and was no longer staring into space.

The woman glanced at the old wives, who nodded. She turned back to the white woman and said, "Why are you bothering me? What do you want?"

No answer. The old wives shrugged their shoulders and pointed to the next suggestion: *Begone, banshee, begone.*

"Begone, banshee, begone!"

The white woman stared with curious pale eyes at the red woman. "Why should I? You're half dead already."

What beautiful eyes, the red woman thought, tipping the contents of her glass down her throat and sucking in her breath at the burn.

THREE

oday, I walked the whole of the house. It was like nosing through a neighbour's or a stranger's house, as there's always something different, like there's some sort of quantum leap and it's an alternative reality of home, but in sections. New staircases appear; new rooms materialise.

This morning, I discover a narrow staircase at the back. I'm sure I never knew about this. The fading wood holds a smell that flashes me back to childhood visits of musty Tudor halls. Familiar, yet unfamiliar. So, as I walk up the stairs, my hand on the banister railing, I feel like I'm holding the hand of a strange old woman, who points with a crooked yet comforting finger, guiding me along a new way. My feet stumble at the unfamiliar depth of the stairs, and the quiver in my thighs jolts me back in time to stumbling sports days, fervent climbing and stage-fright adrenaline.

It's times like these I wonder if I am in my home, the house I think I know, and then suddenly I see something different. I arrive in a new room and my heart lifts. Here is all that was lost of my childhood.

Rows upon rows of shelves house my entire lifetime of books. All the books I have ever had, all the books I have ever read, ever known, are all here gloriously together in one room. Safe. I look back at these tales as a parent might a lost baby. My body aches with knowing I must have, surely, once held them, but having no solid presence to confirm the memory sends the ache into a bewildered doubt. I *had* known them. I *had* held them, *hadn't* I?

I scan the shelves, pluck books out at random and revel in covers I'd forgotten until now. Embossed faces and animals rise beneath my fingertips, the colours seeping into long-neglected areas of my memory. I am starved by the fade of time. I struggle to sustain a whole picture with only fragments of half-remembered colours and tales.

I move between choked shelves, always looking, always seeking, until I come across a lost baby and the joy overtakes the search. I clutch the lost treasure with both hands, then, bit by bit, I let my fingers stroke the cover, like feelers sniffing out the story, forgotten moments restored through a tangible presence. Yet these moments bloom into a fullness that jars when it culminates to a point. Missing. There's something missing.

There is still one baby to seek. One golden child amidst the others.

Why can't I find this? I just know—I *know* I had it. It definitely wasn't a library book. Damn, I even remember the bookshop I got it from, and now *that's* no longer there. Not that it would be any use it still being there. It was a second-hand bookshop, so the chances of the bookseller remembering this book are pretty slim.

But I know I had it. Have it? It's in here somewhere, for sure, but the top shelves are so high I can't reach them.

I need something to climb on, a stepladder or something. Hey, one of those slidy library ladders would be the thing! But where on earth would I get one of those?

I stand and look about and up at the rows of shelves full of books. My stomach gurgles like it's full of roiling spring coils. I need to eat. This will have to wait for another time. I can't reach the top shelves anyway, and it must be hours since I last ate and drank. I drink in one more view of the books as I whisper goodbye. I know they answer me.

The kitchen is right down at the bottom of the house and at the end of an old passage. Sunlight streams in from the large windows, which open onto the garden. I expect my dad to walk in any minute for a cup of tea and a cheese and tomato butty after doing some digging or planting. He'd always ask if I wanted one too. Just cheese for me. I didn't like tomatoes back then, not like now. Now I eat them like apples.

I wasn't an overly sensitive child at school, especially infant school, I'm sure I was quite hard. Brisk. Maybe even tough. Not unfeeling; I just didn't cry as much as the others. I remember one day, in infants, we were milling around the classroom learning about plants, looking at the ones in the window bottom and also in The Growing Corner. I remember the sun streaming in—large windows surrounded us, so we always got hot and quite smelly. I was trying to do something, I can't think what exactly, and I was sweaty and sticky, and a butterfly kept flapping under my nose— perhaps enjoying the plants (although I didn't think that at the time, otherwise I probably wouldn't have done what I did), perhaps trying to fit through the window.

Anyway, I killed it. Just like that. I squashed it with my bare hand. I remember a smudge of reddish-brown on the thumb pad of my right palm. I didn't give it a second thought, and then someone started crying, and then another one—that boy with the pudding-bowl hair of a greyish colour like dodgy faeces was crying and pointing at me, then the dead butterfly. A girl with red cheeks who was always fiddling with her knickers stood behind him, screaming with her eyes tight shut. I thought she couldn't know what she was crying for; the stupid thing she couldn't even see. And then I said that to her, and she screamed even louder.

I looked at the butterfly on the windowsill and remember not knowing what to say, so I scraped it up and put it in my dress pocket. I told the crying children I would bury it later and they could come to the funeral if they wanted. I thought this would comfort them, and then I left them alone. Later, when we were all sitting at our tables, I looked in my pocket at the butterfly tucked into a dusty corner. It hadn't moved. I had stilled it, but I hadn't got rid of it; I could never do that.

I walked home from school and found Dad in his study. I silently took the butterfly from my pocket and put it on his desk. I told him I'd killed it and made the others cry. A wave of emotion caught me, and I started weeping, and Dad asked why I was crying. I said I felt sad, and he asked, "Because of the butterfly?" I nodded and said it was also because I wasn't upset at the time like the others.

I know what pudding-bowl and twisty-knickers would do if that happened now: they wouldn't twitch an eyelid.

And I would feel even sadder than the moment I placed those broken wings on my father's desk.

*

I wash down the last crumbs of my sandwich with some fresh, cool water and rest my head on the kitchen table. The earthy, solid wood is comforting against my forehead, and the kitchen is wonderfully quiet. Only the musical interruptions of birdsong...

*

The tourist village was set back in pale beige rock, smelling of chip fat, ice cream and the hot breath of laughter and family arguments. The arrangement of the sickly rock construction led one around in a fashion to allow successive access to all attractions, but like all tourist parks, there were odd moments of multiple choice. The pathway of beige boulders pattered onwards like a brooch spotted with glittering circles arranged in a manner of ornament rather than utility. And now these rocks trotted around in circles that dared to allow the visitor a personal authority.

At this point, the group broke up; two others and I went into a small arcade containing three small shops. I stepped down some craggy beige steps and through a turnstile into a beautiful-smelling shop. I stood still for a moment to breathe in the scent, then walked towards a table which held sweets, flapjacks and incense. I sniffed the incense and admired the huge variety of sweets, but my attention was drawn to the jams. They were stacked on a large dresser, little checked hats on their lids. I went to look closer at another table arranged with notebooks and small editions of poetry, yet before I reached it, the futility in looking around a shop of this kind washed over me. I had no children to whom I could give presents, so why enter a toyshop?

The colourful jam had disappeared, and the dresser was cluttered with gaudy wooden trains and puppets, flapjacks and incense—no. Card games and marbles. The shop was lined with red and blue and green and yellow, with no modulations of colour, no variation of intensity, just a flat presence of train after boat after puppet after car.

I felt obliged to look around, though, as I had chosen to come into this shop. I headed for a corner loaded with toys textured with fur and felt and plastic, rather than the void wooden creations. As I moved forward, I noticed five shop assistants closing in—I had no room to escape and had to continue toward the toys. One smiling shop assistant waited in the corner for me, and he showed me toy after toy, after game after game, but wait! I turned the handle on a small, blue square of plastic with a tiny screen on the front. As the handle turned, scratchy-looking animals slowly leapt along the screen. This was much better, and I pumped the handle faster to admire the vast selection of animals packed into one little blue plastic case. Before my eyes, the animals grew, and the colours developed and cleared. Oh, look at this one—to the shop assistants standing over me. The fish was so large that as I pumped the handle faster, slowly, the head revealed itself, faster, faster, gradually emerging and growing. I turned the handle furiously, the fish now so massive its body was bursting out of the screen in a fleshy, smooth, thick mass, and I turned and turned. The shop assistants looked at one another. She doesn't know, they thought.

"We must warn you," they said. "Once the tail reveals itself, the fish will gain life."

"Okay," I said, and I turned and turned, pumping the handle as a sweat broke out on my head.

She doesn't understand, *they thought.*

They don't understand, *I thought.*

The slippery flesh pressed and dipped, growing and leaping as quickly as the bulging meat would allow.

*

I wake up. I can smell the fish, and I can smell the paint seeped into the thick mass of flesh. I sit up straight at the kitchen table, inhaling the pungent scent. It fills me with a sense of dread—foreboding, perhaps—but I try to embrace it, to accept it. I inhale and notice a small blob in the doorway. A blob of green and blue. I watch it change shape as I stare just past it, then stand up and walk towards it. As I bend towards the green and blue blob, I realise it is a wooden train. I pick it up and carry it into the hall. Splashes of paint dot the carpet, and I step into the pools of green and blue and yellow and red. I feel the paint thinly squirt between my toes, and I press them into the carpet while I follow the trail down the hall and up a flight of stairs.

I wander the house, opening the panelled doors a crack and letting the rooms spread out before me. They are all I need. They are now more a parent's embrace than anything else I can have.

Unless my hidden book would show itself.

FOUR

own the road, in the nearby town, the red woman sat straight in her armchair, eyes cast towards a corner of the ceiling as the earth turned and shadows cast a virescent light on her white walls. She soaked herself in the green gleam, enjoying the curious hue the curtains threw on her skin. The green changed shade as the day and night developed and grew, reminding her of the passage and circularity of time. She watched the colours. She watched and watched. She watched until she realised there was more than one colour in a colour.

She appreciated the life in lifeless things; the intangible greens titillated her room with their movements. She sustained the unsustainable and revelled in the changing patterns her efforts allowed. She sat in her armchair and watched how she had manipulated the effect of nature and created a room of green. And when she had watched enough, she read her words in the air and laughed at their prettiness.

She moved around in her kitchen, humming softly. In the other room, the white woman still sat, straight-faced and upright. The red woman continued with her preparations, sometimes pausing to allow her thoughts to trickle down her body, to become rooted in her tissue, her muscles; to have time to seep outwards into her arms, hands, fingernails; to sparkle and drip from her fingertips so that each time she put her hand to her face, her head, the idea glitters would be processed once again.

After a while, the red woman came and sat and looked at her banshee. She couldn't imagine her flat now without her; she'd become something of a pet. Her room bathed in green enhanced the whiteness of the seated figure, her pallid hands folded in her lap. It was curious where she'd come from, but the dreadfully white woman didn't seem to know herself, and the red woman wasn't worried about it. In fact, her arrival had been surprisingly welcome.

"More wine, I think," she said to the figure. The white woman did not answer but continued to gaze at the red woman.

"I'll just go and get some from the kitchen." She walked out of the room and brought back a second bottle of red wine, uncorked it and swirled the open neck in a circle under her nose. "You must let it breathe for a little while."

While she was waiting, the woman went up to the banshee and poured some of the drink onto the wall next to her. The red trickled down, leaving a pink stain. Then she took the bottle with her to the chair and sat looking across the room at the pattern she had created. "You really are deathly white, you know." The red woman burst out into laughter. "But that splash of pink complements you beautifully, darling."

It was so refreshing, so...*vindicating*, to have a canvas to work with. Perhaps this was what she'd needed all along. The red woman leant back and trailed a hand across the arm of her chair. She peered at the white woman glowing bright against the pink stain. Was this why she'd appeared? A strange thought—that someone had come to her for this after all those years of no appreciation, no recognition.

A butterfly of wondering tickled her face. *Where did the white woman come from?* But it had flown away before she could even look at it. And besides, it was time to do some shopping. That had become necessary.

*

Waitrose. Low roof, white tiles discernible only by the grainy black lines separating each lump from the other, and that hum found in supermarkets, hospitals, public libraries. The red woman moved through it like a symphony.

She went to the checkout, loaded her contents onto the dusty black belt and watched the bottle of red wine, the bag of mushrooms, the wedge of cheese and the packet of pistachios fade away before retrieving them in an ugly plastic bag.

The people in the queue were smiling, grumpy, impatient, bored, busy. There is something so lovely about supermarkets. Everybody speaks to the checkout operator; they smile and perhaps say hello. A big flashy grin or a shy movement of the lips. It doesn't matter if they're fake. It might have mattered once. Now she has her own canvas.

By the time she had wandered back home, it was late, yet inside the green room, it was as always, just a slightly darker shade. She opened her wine and curled up in her chair opposite the white woman.

Sitting, drinking, watching, thinking.

Later. Still drinking and watching. The eyes of the two women had connected across the room, the link between gazes reaching like a cool, steel staff. Something travelled along the staff like a trickle of electricity, but the loop was broken as the red woman stood with a sigh and snapped the rod.

Stretching her body with cat-like languor, she went across to the bookcase and picked out a volume. She stroked it absentmindedly, like a beard or a small pet, enjoying the smoothness until the rhythmic effect of the touch seemed to become part of her own circadian rhythm. She looked at some more covers on the books, then slid them back into place.

When she had looked at every one, she took the book with the most beautiful cover over to the white woman and held it in front of her face. Silence. Peeking around the book, the red woman whispered in the other's ear, "Do you not think it the most divine covering?"

The white woman looked directly into her eyes.

"Oh, my dear, you must learn to appreciate beauty."

Silence.

"Your mind is empty for lack of visual stimulation. You cannot imagine."

Silence still.

"I can teach you—" straightening up "—I will show you." She laughed and laughed as she looked at the white woman.

"You always look so bloody serious. It's a shame, really. It could spoil your pretty eyes."

The red woman pottered and tottered, a fizz of purpose bubbling up in her stomach as colours and shapes played before her eyes.

The banshee sat and looked at the woman who soaked her body with red, and as she watched, her eyes became as bloody as the contents of the glass. As bloody, and as watery.

FIVE

eyond the lake and below the rough hills of Flora, there was the small town of the red woman. The town was quiet and rather beautiful. And although the town was quiet, it was busy. All times of the day saw people coming and going, browsing and working, drinking tea and lugging shopping bags. Yet when the eye took time to notice, it saw that the town was both busy and quiet. There was a noticeable proportion of women there. They governed the day, which cast its light on this multitude of females who shaded their eyes from the glare and covered their heads with plastic nets when the sky scattered a drop of nourishment. The town held meetings, ran a newspaper, had several associations—and it guarded these with a jealous privacy.

The one point of unity lay in the belly of the Universal Mother: the goddess who sat over the town. And then there were smaller offshoots of oneness: the coffee mornings and crèche groups were small feats of architecture to come about from this common existence. The beautiful town held them all in its palm.

The people worked hard in each their own way, and they liked to keep to themselves. The men were tired and looked forward to their papers, their armchairs and their model ships. The women had the luxury of extra time and strength, and they looked forward to their community, the building of their sect.

*

The red woman occasionally felt the urge to go out into society, to mingle with other people and see what they were wearing. She felt that today. She put on her red felt hat, the one with a burgundy flower on the rim, and her black floral dress. She stood in front of the mirror for a long time fluffing up the sleeves. They were a beautiful, silk, split cut. The red woman stood, barefoot, frilling and preening as the minutes ticked past. She had been up half the night anyway, so what now felt like late afternoon was, in fact, early morning.

She put on her shoes and went downstairs and out into the street. The breeze flapped up her arms, and she smiled at the freshness. She walked around the town for an hour, feeling the air on her bare arms. The glances of other people fed her; their attention nourished her. "I really am a people-person," she said to herself. She paused to look in a shop window and then, as she was feeling so sociable, decided to go for a drink in the café. She sat by the window to watch the people go by, running her finger around and around the rim of her glass.

In the corner of the café, three women had watched the woman in the floral dress come in and sit down. Their eyes rebounded like colliding billiard balls. "Yes, that's her, for sure," the fattest woman, Mrs. D, said after a few minutes. "I haven't seen her for a while, but it's definitely her. She's not long ago moved in up the road."

"Oh, it's been a few years, surely," the thinnest woman, Mrs. F, said.

"Well, it's so hard to know for sure, when somebody doesn't mingle with the community," remarked the middle-sized woman, Mrs. M.

"Yes, yes, but I'm sure, too, she's been in the town for a few years now." Mrs. D nodded to Mrs. F. "I'm sure you're right, dear."

"Well, I say she's an odd 'un," said Mrs. M. "She moves here, she doesn't mix with folk, and yet she thinks she belongs. She's got a cheek, for sure."

"Oh, you're right. Just look at her, sipping her wine there like Lady Muck."

"Probably living off her husband's assets."

"Probably bumped him off to get them."

"No!"

The three women turned to look at the red woman, who sat looking out of the window. She had taken off her hat, and her hair twisted down over her shoulders in black coils. She smiled at the people going to and fro along the cobbled street. And so, four women sat in the café, three looking at one, who looked out onto the town.

SIX

s time passed, the red woman found tasks to do throughout her days and nights. She was finally a master of her own creations—a role she'd coveted but never quite managed to acquire. And the white woman was so accepting of all this! She sat back and watched the show, and the red woman was propelled forward by her new audience.

She was so busy, in fact, she only left her house when necessary, rushing to the shops with her head down to see how quickly her feet were going. Grab, smile, pay, smile, and rush back.

She became so absorbed in her current project she temporarily forgot the presence of the other woman. Her project was a splendid sculpture in the middle of the room, with ten hardback books in varying shades of blue for a base. The red woman had delighted in creating a rainbow of one colour then running her hand over the smooth fronts of the books, feeling the tingly warmth from the electric blue, the velvet softness of the purple and the refreshing comfort of a small square sky. She thrilled, knowing a myriad of words lay settled beneath this rainbow.

She collected ten empty wine bottles, all of green glass, and placed one on each book. Beautiful green against varying hues of blue.

She loved to concentrate on each individual segment of the rainbow and study the effect of different blues against the same green. A plank of wood next, teetering along the necks of the wine bottles. She positioned a big old vase in the middle of the plank. The colour wasn't quite right, but that could be fixed. So, for the moment, a bland magnolia vase rested on the plank; she was reluctant to remove it and disrupt her creation, although the bland ugliness increasingly disturbed her.

She dreamt incessantly about it that night, tossing over and waking up every fifteen minutes, the image taunting her eyes regardless of if they were closed or open. At last, she could bear it no longer and got out of bed, determined to find something to transform the object. Leaving her shoulders bare, she went downstairs in her nightdress.

As she passed the kitchen, she caught sight of her leftover wine. "A bit of inspiration oil? Don't want a slap-dash job, after all." She took her large glass into the room with the offending vase and took a sip. "Now then, what have we got?" Scrutinising the room in one swoop, she jumped when the white figure in the corner caught her eye. "What the—oh! It's you. I'd forgotten all about you, darling. What are you doing up? Do you never sleep?" The banshee stared vacantly at the ruffled woman. "Well, whatever. I must do something about this vase, so don't disturb me."

She knelt in front of her sculpture and weighed it up. Then, going over to the bookcase, she chose a few books with pretty jackets and removed the sleeves. She sat and arranged the coloured sleeves around the vase, tucking the new colour into the neck and mouth and dressing the fat body with the thick paper. She arranged it so the book covers fell in thick crumples and creases, the shadows evoking a quality of soft material. She folded and tucked, smoothed and scrunched, until the magnolia jar appeared to be draped in sumptuous velvet.

As the sun rose on her endeavours, the green cast from the curtains fell on the sculpture, catching in the bottles and reflecting onto the rainbow of blue. The woman sat with stained lips smiling at her creation, feeling calm and settled. She could sleep for a while now. And so, she slept. And her mind was blank.

*

When the woman woke, rain was pouring down. She sprawled out, listening to it pelt the roof. After a few minutes, the tiny hammers broke through and started chiselling into her head. She sucked in her breath as she stumbled to look for some painkillers and groaned when she realised there were none. She decided to go and see her neighbours to borrow some and staggered down the road in her bare feet.

She stood at the door in her nightdress with red, cracked lips and pungent breath. While the neighbour went to fetch the tablets, the red woman wandered upstairs and saw a small girl playing with dolls in her bedroom.

"How beautiful!"

The girl turned and smiled. "Why are you in your nightie? It's nearly teatime."

"Oh, I don't know." The red woman stepped into the room and went and sat next to the girl. "What lovely dolls."

"Yes, I know. I'm dressing them up for the disco." The girl carried on brushing one of the dolls' hair.

"Delightful! What time does it start?"

"Six o'clock."

"Goodness, that's early. We must hurry to get them ready." The red woman picked up a doll with long, reddish-brown hair and started to undress her. How strange, that she'd not paid this much attention before to her daughter's dolls. She scratched her nostril carefully. Had she *had* dolls like this, though? She mustn't have, because she and her daughter would have spent time doing this. Perhaps that had been part of the problem—not the right props.

ORIGINS

SEVEN

I saunter around my garden with the sun on my face and stoop to smell the lavender. The colours vary so much and yet complement each other; all these differences together, the more variations the better. That deep violet next to the shower of yellow, the purple so fragile at the edges, almost like bat's ears, transparent illuminated skin, then deeper into the trumpet as it darkens. The colour is always there, just progressively different.

I reach forward to touch it, and as I stroke the floral velveteen, my eyes swim lazily over the garden. A rose, a beautiful solitary rose amidst a tangle of green and brown; pink against green, just a small dot, but enough to create an impact...

A solitary thing of beauty is more beautiful than a mass of the same.

A solitary thing of beauty evinces more strength than a multitude of dependants.

Solitude is beautiful as a consequence of its uniqueness.

One thing does make a difference in this world.

*

There is that heaviness again. The air hangs laden with the essence of lavender and wet trees, barely leaving room for bodies to pass beneath it. Heavy and fragrant. The birdsong alone can penetrate this thick-smelling air; it catches in the closeness and spreads itself like musical blood rushing through veins.

Everything is weighty, so full—the beauty is almost stifling. Almost *too* rich. The masses of leafy green dip into the musk, and scent seeps into the plant as watercolour into tissue. Now even breezes are loaded. They drift into the verdant, perfumed layers and rest for a moment in the pungent mass, struggling under the combined density to lift the leaves with a weak puff.

Olive turns to emerald as streaks of saffron rest and dissolve. There is the atmosphere of contingency, of waiting, of ending, and it never happens. It is secured in the weight. It has swallowed time and so hangs, bloated, its presence almost tangible but never discernible. It teases but never happens.

*

The darkness begins to sink into the garden like water into a sponge, the colours fade almost to a monochrome until it's like I'm sitting in an old postcard. The breeze becomes chilly, so I get my coat from the side porch and then set off through the garden onto the rough path to the main road across the hills. This was the path my dad would take, late in the evening when he thought I was tucked up asleep.

The breeze is scented with nightfall and rubs against the gravel, which crunches and rolls as I walk. My mind is distant yet simple, like a crafted stone wrapped in fleece, my thoughts so far away I must unravel the sheep's wool and nettle sting to remember the semi-precious gem I am polishing. I enjoy unpacking it and then ravelling it in yet more layers of peat, heather, ragged hair caught on barbed wire, until it's wound so tight, I am lost in that forgotten place again and my mind swings around inside my head.

Walk. Just keep walking. It'll stop soon.

And it does.

I pause for a while as I pass the dip that holds a farmhouse in its nest. I love to see the warmth of the lights and the warmer glow of the life glimpsed through the windows. But beauty is defiant. In the yard, two old Robin Reliants sit rotting.

One white. The other green. Both are in various stages of deterioration, the white three-wheeler covered in rust, mould and patches of flaked paint. The flat tyres give a slug-like quality to the immobile machine. Many people would claim it an ugly sight, yet a laburnum flowers over the roof of the old car in a shower of gold, tickling the wasted body, and pink roses at the top of the wall rest in a cluster.

Whether the car emphasises the beauty of the flowers or the flowers heighten the loveliness of the banger, I don't know, but the two together are stunning.

I reach the Olde Pheasant. The dots of orange glow that had winked at me across the hills are now in front of me, warm, welcoming. Like a real home.

Inside, a few regulars up from town enjoy a quiet beer, some passers-by take a break from a journey, and a couple of farmers rest and drink. The owners don't mind serving me—I'm no trouble to them or the other older ones. A young face is rare here, and I think they enjoy my innocence. This is one place where people can be comfortable in silence, talking only when conversation naturally arises.

The cellarman works here in the mornings and comes in every evening for ale and company. If he's needed through the night, he gets up and leaves his half-full glass while he goes to change a barrel. Task completed, he resumes drinking. He has worked here for as long as I can remember and says he's known me from a baby, but my only recollection of him when I was very young is an earthy smell of sweet tobacco and wet grass. Tonight, I sit next to him. It is lovely and warm in the Pheasant. Orange and brown warmth.

"You okay, Turnip?" the cellarman asks.

I crinkle up inside. He's always called me Turnip. I nod. "Are you?"

"Oh, yes. Always. Always on the middle road, you know. Let me get you a drink of something refreshing. That's a long walk you do over those moors."

"It's not so bad. But thanks. Are you sure? I'll have an orange with ice, please."

The cellarman, Bob to other people, points a finger to the fridge behind the bar and nods to the landlord. "With ice, too, Geoff."

The drink is glorious. The cool juice trickles down and pools in the pit of my stomach as the insides of my cheeks glitter with the trinkets of ice I'm crunching.

"So what've you been doing today then, Turnip?"

"Um…" What have I been doing? For a split second, my mind spins again; it's so difficult to remember. "I don't think I've done much, actually. Just pottering about the house."

"Don't you fancy getting out a bit more? Into town and meet some other young 'uns?"

I purse my lips at him. Doesn't he know me at all? "No. I'm happy doing my thing."

"Ah. Of course." He takes a healthy swig from his pint and rolls his lips together to squeeze the froth into his mouth. "Happy doing your thing. And erm, what is 'your thing'? Everybody has one. Mostly everybody. Mine is tending to my bees and coming here."

My thing.

My eyes feel crystal clear looking into his. "Well, pottering—that's my thing, I guess. Well, no—exploring, actually!"

His smile is a comforting crumple of weathered skin and deep lines. "Exploring? Well, that is a great thing. You've plenty of space to explore, for sure." His crumples release suddenly as he peers at me with deep brown eyes. "And what have you discovered?"

What have I discovered? There's so much I don't know where to start. "I've discovered…sometimes I can't seem to find what it is exactly I'm searching for, as there is so much else along the way. I seem to get…distracted…" I trail my words into my orange.

"Oh. Yes, I understand. Well, there is the greatest exploration of all. You've got yourself quite a bit of work cut out there, Turnip."

EIGHT

he red woman was still in her nightie with the little girl as they sat playing dolls. The hammers had stopped banging, and she concentrated intently on decorating her doll.

"You should put a dress on yours if we are going to a party," Sara said as the woman dressed her doll in a suit. "She can't wear that. It's not for girls."

"As long as she looks beautiful, it doesn't matter if they are men's clothes. And she does look beautiful, doesn't she?"

"Hmmm, I'm not sure. She doesn't look like a girl."

"But she *is* a girl, and this *is* beautiful. That's all that should matter. What if she were to look like a girl and yet wear something ugly? No, far better like this."

Sara nodded and sat very quietly, dressing her doll.

When it was time for the girl to have a bath and go to bed, the woman lingered, thinking about her empty house. She wasn't meant to be alone; she was destined for society, for company, for limelight. For a horrifying moment, she was transported back in time, cut out from the loop, looking for appreciation from people who didn't understand her. She thought she'd escaped that.

But on remembering her newly created sculpture, she skipped up the road. She saw she had left her lights on. She could see movement inside her house. She'd forgotten! She'd forgotten that woman in her home. That white woman who sat and stared, all white and colourless and speechless. Gosh, what was she doing putting up with a thing like that in her home?

She felt panic smothering her. She wasn't free. She was being swamped and suffocated and—wait! She had made her sculpture. It was hers and hers only; a fragment of her self. She must finish it, add to it, still so much she could do, and she could do it despite the awful presence of that woman, that white woman who sat and stared and got whiter and whiter and whiter...wait. Could she paint her? Dim the brightness, and with the brightness dimmed, carry on as before?

She stopped at the door as she thought and then laughed. What was she doing? This was her house, her home, her sculpture, her books, her wine—why so scared? She laughed and laughed as she opened the door and went in. "Hi, honey, I'm home!" she bellowed at the top of her voice. The woman charged up the stairs to her sitting room, then paused. She could take control of this. The white woman would appreciate her for it, too.

Smiling, she went into the kitchen cupboard and sought out some tins of paint. Crimson, lilac and yellow ochre. She sauntered into the lounge with the tins of paint tucked under her arms and set them down on a table. Dabbing a brush into the lilac, she strolled over to the white woman, humming. "Right, if you're going to stop in my house,

it's about time you started fitting in with one or two things."
She raised the brush to the other woman's face, droplets of
paint dripping onto her own feet.

As she tried to dab the paint onto the woman's cheeks,
the brush went straight through onto the wall. She knelt
down to paint the white ankle, yet the bristles swept the
chair. The red woman stood up and glared at the white
woman, then stormed over to the tins of paint. She prised
the lids off the crimson and the yellow and flung them over
the pale figure. "You ugly bitch!" she screamed. The paint
splattered against the pale walls like a burning sunset, and
still the banshee sat white, stark, piercing the other woman
with her gaze.

The red woman plonked into the armchair and stared
back at the banshee, the glaring whiteness of her, and the
splurge of crimson and ochre on the wall. She would not
be defeated by this imposing figure. No, she would use
the woman's pale colouring to her advantage, and if this
speechless banshee refused to be art herself, she would
position art around her. Satisfied with her decision, she
closed her eyes and dreamt of wonderful castles made from
ribbons and bubble wrap.

*

*Look at her...half passed out to the world and herself...when
is she going to go? Why was I sent here and yet she lingers?
When is she going to go? I don't know how long I'll have to stay
here...if she doesn't go soon...she's crazy too...there's some peace
now she's sleeping...*

*

The next morning, the woman woke early and went into the town. It was quieter than when she usually went in yet more busy, as people trotted, rather than meandered, by. It was a curious quiet business. The people were absorbed in their own world, their eyes glassy, unseeing to anything except the business inside them.

Tall, bony women, squat men with suits and baby faces, fat women with big black handbags. They huffed and waddled, taking little notice of the beauty in the town, the painted buildings, the old streets.

The toll of ten o'clock saw three stout women gather in the town centre. Mrs. M, Mrs. F and Mrs. D met one another with a greeting emitted deep from the bowels of habit. No ringing joy, no resentful obligation, just involuntary movement towards each other.

The clock spewed its regular belchings over the town, reminding folk where they were, when, why, yet never who. These routine janglings endeavoured to tell them who they were—the whole of a life encased in a greening bronze bell that blurted across the land with no shame for privacy.

And so Mrs. M, Mrs. F and Mrs. D met. They walked with great purpose to the café on the corner of the street, at the bottom of a beautiful, twisted cobbled hill. Mrs. M and Mrs. D sat at a table while Mrs. F ordered three teas.

They sipped their tea. They opened up their bodies for the tepid drink to enter and explore their system. Their puckered lips formed a cracked tunnel for the liquid to travel down. The secret to tea drinking is the curl of the lips, the wrinkled pucker. Mrs. M, Mrs. F and Mrs. D puckered and quivered as their eyes penetrated the room with a steady, low line of sight.

After half an hour of casting their scrutiny over the inexperienced tea drinkers of the shop (who swallowed with full, plump lips), Mrs. M, Mrs. F and Mrs. D contracted their gaze into a small circle, a circle of three, heads down, eyes up and lips exquisitely formed to an 'o'. Their fertile goddess sits over them, guiding their tea drinking, their tongues, their bodies.

The women sat and discussed their children, the heartache and arguments with one another. They felt their woman's tradition; a mother's tradition. They talked together about bowel movements, pubescent manners, increased washing loads and nodded and sipped together. It has all been—it all is—worthwhile when it means they can congregate and talk in a like-minded manner before their goddess, the Universal Mother.

The Universal Mother presides over them, their talk, their maternity, and they look up to her, try to emulate her. No one questions the presence of the Universal Mother. No one questions the existence of her, for it would question their vocation and destroy their womanly tradition. They would have nothing special to mark them out, no uterine wisdom. How they long for the world to see their uterine wisdom.

"It's a question of work," Mrs. M said. "Hard work. It's not easy being a mother—it's a full-time job. My girl doesn't know she's born, thinks it's a given right she should go out, have holidays."

"Hm, yes. They do, though, they do."

"I say to her, 'By gad, girl, you've got some learning to do.'"

"Hm, yes, hm, they do, don't they?"

"And her boyfriend—he should leave well alone and let a woman get on with her work, never mind interfering."

"Oh, yes, yes."

"Yes, it's only natural, isn't it?"

"Mother knows best, that's what I say. It's written in her milk."

NINE

he red woman had been thinking. It was futile trying to beautify the white woman. All her efforts were in vain.

And she'd been thinking about the ugliness in the world and its desperate need for something. Some wonder, some colour. People were so blind to any beauty around them, they simply couldn't notice what was under their noses, or above their heads, or under their feet.

And she'd been thinking: it's not enough for just one person to make beauty; it needs to live on. So she had been thinking about having a child. A child of beauty and creativity and appreciation. She could create that and mould it, teach it, nurture it. She could decorate it herself and create a living, breathing piece of beauty.

And this time, she was focused; she had shaken off her old dry existence and was determined not to fail.

All she needed was a man. Well, rather, some sperm. She wondered where to get it from. It had to be beautiful sperm, of course, and from a beautiful situation. No, she couldn't get it now; not now it had drifted into autumn.

The right sperm wasn't here yet. She would have to wait for the spring.

She could think, in the meantime, of the beautiful life she would mould when her daughter was born. For it had to be a daughter. What could she possibly drape around a saggy old penis to render it an object of awe? She dragged her quilt down from her bed and hugged it around her in the chair, surrounding the base with bottles of wine. She sucked on a corkscrew as she watched the dancing light on the walls through the green curtains.

As she sipped and slurped, she looked at the pretty pictures floating from her head. They slapped onto the wall in front of her and played their part before her eyes. She had made these pictures; they were hers and yet there for all to see. She shifted excitedly at the thought of inviting Sara over to see her sculpture, her dancing words, her motion picture of thoughts. She could talk to her while waiting for her sperm to arrive. Still, for the moment she was content, sitting snug in her quilt, drinking quietly while she allowed her sensations to take form.

TEN

The town had shrunk down to a milky set as the moon appeared. Colours had withdrawn into doors and hallways as shadows cast over the pavements, streets, buildings, until all was transformed into a still darkness, save for the cosy glow of street- and lamplights.

Families nestled in their cocoons; groups congregated in pubs or church meetings. Mrs. M, Mrs. F and Mrs. D met weekly to knit. The pitch of their voices ran deep as they searched into the baggage of themselves for forgotten, pilfered pearls. They were not worked from their own lives but a slight peripheral around them. Gossip. Other women. Teachers. Books.

The form of the female body allowed them, however, to assume a sister voice and take on her load. Mrs. M, the fattest, must be crammed full of pearls. Weekly, she spewed them out to feed her pack.

Mrs. F and Mrs. D used Mrs. M's wisdom to highlight their own. Their nods and uh-huhs to Mrs. M's maxims testified their own intuition.

The Universal Mother sits high above them as they talk, flavouring their speech with her own milk. They acknowledge her incessantly; they worship her; after all, she verifies their existence and their way of life. She makes them real.

The men of the town stand at the bar, eyes forward while they talk into their pints, or the washing-up bowl if they stay at home. Their wisdom is a hard-earned gem, a jewel cultivated from the rough. There is no Father, though, no all-seeing, all-knowing Father who speaks through his myriad of sons, permeating their self with his presence, his mark.

Mrs. F sat back and recounted her rows. "Our Sara's been playing with that woman up the road," she said. "Like a child herself, she is."

"Odd, more like," said Mrs. M. "Curtains always closed. Makes you think she's got something to hide."

"No, she's nothing to hide. More like an open book, if you speak to her. Sara told me she's wanting a baby."

"A baby?" said Mrs. M. "But she's no fella to speak of. Unless she's hiding one behind them closed curtains." She winked at Mrs. D, who chuckled. The idea of that woman taking part in such a sacred ritual held a comic sobriety for the three women, who then sauntered into accounts of childbirth, personal, related and mythical. The pain flowing from their bodies was a form of wisdom, an initiation rite. They knew their own bodies. They knew each other's bodies. They passed this knowledge on to one another from mouth to mouth like a precious egg. The egg of the Universal Mother. Yet never the yolk, only the shell. The women thrived on keeping the shell unbroken, the centre contained.

Mrs. M drifted onto the topic of her daughters and sons. She despairs, she said. She wonders where she has gone wrong and doesn't know what to say to them. She'd warned them, she said. Mrs. F and Mrs. D nodded their heads wisely.

"And he's not much use," she said.

"Oh, no, no," Mrs. F and Mrs. D said. "You have to do it all on your own."

They hmm-ed and nodded and clicked and clacked with their needles, their eyes resting on one another, settling into each other, their laughter threading across the room like a web. As the web thickened and tangled, they chomped their way through it, biting into the rich fruit they had placed in the gossamer frame.

ELEVEN

he red woman had barely shifted from her armchair. Her opposite wall was now full of colours, lines and images, and she could hardly move. They were almost confusing, but it was busy, and it had been a lot of hard work. She gave a yelp.

"Sara! I must show her all my beauties!" And she stretched over to the phone. "No, on second thoughts, I'll call in...no, I'll ring her." She nodded and dialled. "Oh. Sara dear, it's you. You must come over. I have so much to show you."

"Hiya. Now?"

"Yes, now, and you must bring over some of your beautiful dolls."

"Okay, but I'll have to finish my tea first and then ask Mum."

"Don't be long. Do you have to have your meal now?"

"Well, yes. It's teatime, isn't it? You can have yours at the same time, and then we'll both be ready together."

"Hmmmm, I'm not sure I'll do that. I'm just too busy. I'll be waiting here."

The red woman put the phone on the floor and lay back in her chair, knees up to her chin. She watched the fading sun through the curtains melt the room into a glow of gold algae, then drape over the ten wine bottles into a sea of green-blue books. She sucked in her breath as she noticed the colour of her dress against the molten wash of green, blue and gold. She needed to change. She might want to be noticed, but not because of that!

She ran upstairs, throwing a quick glance at the silent white figure as she went. She threw her clothes on the floor and slid an off-white dress over her body. Cream would enhance the fluid glow in her room and would show that white woman the advantage of toning down such an offensive glare. She ran downstairs and stood with her back to the banshee, so she could admire the shifting beauty of her lounge, untainted by her ghostly figure.

TWELVE

love this turn in the weather. The crispness reminds me of breath puffs and walks across the moor. Things crispen and curl: leaves, cones, branches, even skin. And everything is washed in a new colour, a warm colour to balance out the tightening chill. How I miss my dad when it's like this. He'd guide me to what I need. I could talk through my jumble with him, and he'd organise it for me into a pristine display. Then I'd surely see the thing I'm looking for.

But he's not here to talk to like that, so I have to listen differently. Things become sharper as the birdsong hones its call and splits the white air with strings of well-rehearsed notes which soak into the washes of red, brown and orange. People liken autumn to death. Is this alternating slap across the face and warm soak of colour what it is to die?

My mother would have been horrified by this idea. She thought colour was in life; to her, life *was* colour. Without it, she said, she would perish. But there are so many different types of colour. It does not always stand glaring you in the face. I wonder if all the others who have lived here loved it.

Perhaps the two children in the cellar loved this curling, wrinkling, brown season. I know they liked drawing; the cold would be just the reason to stay indoors and make their mark. Yellow streaks of chalk filling out two sturdy legs, a dash of faded red depicting a wide mouth bleeding with its stifled quietness or perhaps secretly—silently—vibrant.

These children lived here a century or so ago, Dad reckoned. I reckon they're still here. They've left parts of themselves—their drawings—so never quite died. Not really; not fully. I look back in time when I trace their chalk pictures. I can hear them, smell them. And it makes me feel even more longing.

I used to be afraid of the drawings on the cellar wall—why weren't they allowed paper? I used to worry. And so they must have been forced to stand up, locked in. Brother and sister punished for sitting improperly, for eating too hungrily, forced to...to what? Draw pictures of men in wide yellow trousers, spinning hoops and balls, a random apple. A punishment, to have a quiet space to make your mark? To have time to unlock forgotten secrets?

No, I was wrong. I used to shudder at these pictures, but now I am fascinated by the mark of a childhood of freedom. They chose to paint on this indelible canvas. Dad helped me see that. He felt they were happy.

And these children knew secrets, ways of doing things, of opening closed doors. One night, they came to my rescue as I was being chased by werewolves and vampires. My own fault perhaps, for I couldn't resist the temptation of looking at an old castle in the middle of the wilds.

It had seemed so peculiar in the night light—bluish black, with dark, dark streaks of purple—I was compelled to go up and touch the stone, to try the door and look inside, but there was my error: the strange, bluish oak door, silvery in the moonlight, housing a gang of monsters. I turned and ran across the slippery dark grass, yet the wolves were always, always gaining on me and my sluggish, heavy body, so heavy I could barely lift my arms to pump faster. But then the children appeared at my side, and holding onto a hand each, they ran along with me, urging my heavy body towards an arrangement of concrete slabs.

—you must run, they said, *up a slab to take off.*

—to fly?

—they act as a platform to give you lift.

—don't leave me.

—we won't.

Three concrete slabs were coming towards us. We needed to leave hold of hands to each control a runway. I ran heavily up the raised stone and carried on my escape route hovering in the air. I rose and dipped and felt the werewolves snapping at my scrabbling feet, then hurled myself up another slab, pressing my chest into the air to lift my body as far as possible. I dipped again, and this time the vampires snapped at my stomach and legs as I began to drop. I pushed my chest higher.

—I can't stay up like you can, I cried.

—you will, just keep pushing.

—I keep dropping.

—use your stone.

I ran and jumped and rose and dropped and lifted until the blue-black grass was free of slabs and stretched out clean and clear and the wolves and vampires were far back on the blue-black grass peppered with half-raised stone slabs.

They had not bothered to follow this far. They can't come this far. We walked across the moonlit grass, our eyes attracted to the glistening drops of wet. I breathed deeply to steady the rush of blood pumping in my head and looked across at the children. They were calm, walking steadily, their faces fresh and untroubled. I saw my house in the distance and felt safe; yet I was also slow to leave this new patch of space we had flown into tonight.

Sometimes, the comfort we feel from another state of consciousness is more real than anything in our waking life. There are a whole variety of landscapes to escape to. They are *in* our selves. And so, despite the fear, I wanted to keep this moment when I found myself in a clear, clean area of blue-black grass.

THIRTEEN

The children have left me. The sun is starting to rise, and yet the air grows chill. I pull a blanket over me on the settee and settle back on a heap of cushions. I can hear them playing in the cellar, scratching the walls with more chalk. Orange, probably. I close my eyes and watch the sun come up through my eyelids, listening to the sound of the wind up on the hills. The little copse will be full of a chase of coarse leaves now, skittering until they have broken through into a rolling expanse of field upon field.

A bit like me, breaking through from room to room here. Sometimes, now, when I wander around the house, I remember my mother. I can go in and out of many rooms and be distant, forgetting, then something suddenly plops her in front of me. Or I can hear her laughing. Always laughing. She didn't really laugh with me. I used to think she was. But she wasn't. She laughed at herself. With herself. It used to make Dad so happy to hear her laugh; he'd stop what he was doing in the garden and lean forward on his spade, his ear cocked towards the house.

One day, she ran out into his arms, and they fell into the rhododendrons laughing. This used to happen a lot when I was younger, but as I grew up, I noticed it less and less. Dad and I spent more time together, while Mum had a headache. After school and in the holidays, Dad and I would go rambling all over the moor. Mum always had a pain—I wonder we didn't both have one in the neck—and she'd lock herself away for hours.

Dad tried to coax her into coming for a walk. "It'll do you good," he said.

"Good?" she said. "Tramping around swamps and god knows what else, good? Bloody hell, I don't even know why we have to live in this god-awful place. Bloody out of the way, no shops, no people even. Just you two, with your walking and your animals and god knows what." Then she screamed in my dad's face, right up close, so he could probably smell her breath. Then she stormed off.

This started to upset me. I tried to talk to Mum, but she was impossible in a rage. When she was happy, it was almost as though Dad and I didn't exist. I try to remember if she was always like that, but I can't. I don't know what she did with herself—I was usually at school, and when I came home, she kept out of the way. I'd sometimes go looking for her, but I'd usually find something to do along the way.

She spent a lot of time in her bedroom, singing to herself in the mirror or going to the city. Still, what's the point in thinking about this?

I sit down in the window seat on the third floor and trace the leading on the glass. Outside, the bushes move slowly. My dad never moved away from me. He was always there. One Sunday, he found me sitting at the bottom of the garden on the stone table near the bushes. I was watching the thick mass of dark green slowly lift up and down in the breeze like heavy arms through water. The smell at the bottom of the garden was different—darker, deeper, more real.

"It's beautiful, isn't it?" he said. I told him I had started to like peace and quiet. "Yes," he nodded. Then we were silent.

We watched the lull of dark leaves rustling in front of us. It was hypnotising...strangely stilling...then Dad patted me on the knee and said, "Treasure these kinds of moments. They are always there to be found, but not always seen. When your eyes do open, celebrate the sight, because it's a sense that can run deep."

I listened carefully to him, concentrating hard on the words. Dad often spoke in this way. As time went on and I grew bigger, he did so more and more. Or perhaps I began to take more notice. It's something I hurt my head with trying to remember now—trying to remember all his words. I keep thinking I should write them down when they come to me. Put them all together in a collection.

I can only remember one living figure I could trust; only one who has never let me down—Dad. Now he's...passed over, and I miss him, but I'm never alone. He went...I don't know when. I suddenly woke up alone one morning, and for the rest of the day and for the rest of the week, and even now, my dad never comes home, and I alone have this house. My father's last gift to me was the space to breed new lives and the room to roam.

I'm just not sure how ready I am for all of that after all.

FOURTEEN

I sit in my comfy chair, enveloped in soft, thick cushions bulging gently into my sides, my feet propped into a state of airborne laziness on a pouffe. The air in my library is cosy and warm; my arms tingle in the luxury. I could be the lord of a country manor house—get me my tweed jacket!

*

So comfortable. So warm...

*

...they were all wearing giant hats with big floppy brims like waves and a massive knobbly middle teetering on small heads. The hats were orange, yellow, green, red, lots of mustard, and all women wearing them. Women tall and thin and anxious. They had to get out of the room; to get out of the room they had to wear the right colour—no mixing—just one straight colour.

Against the wall, rocking chairs were lined up: pink, red, pink, blue, pink, red, pink, blue. Such order. Chisels and drills on either arm of each chair. The women sat in the chairs and rocked, then took hold of a chisel in one hand, the drill in the other and began to chip-chip-chip and drill through the wood. Hole after hole, after hole, chip, chip, and rocking and whizzing down, working down, rocking down further, and further...

Then there was a butcher, and another, and his scrawny sweaty apprentice, with giant cleavers brandished over their heads. Shiny chunks of metal. The butchers were laughing. I had to get out quick and find one of the women and let her chisel us out of here. Colour sparks flashed in the corner of my eye, but when I looked, they disappeared around a whitewashed corner. I heard laughter—got to get out, a hand clutched my shoulder. A woman in mustard scarves and hats and skirts. She took my hand and ran, leading the way—pant-pant-pant—heart bursting, chest gasping, straining. Quick the chair, sit in it. She sat on my knee and started drilling, whrrrrr, whrrrrr, and you chisel, she said, chip-chip-chip, whrrrrr, chip-chip, whrrrrr.

They send us spinning like the needle of the drill. Quick, there's the butcher. His smiling, fat, rosy face, bristles like snapped beetles' legs sticking out of his chin, and we could smell him. Chip, whrrrrr, chip, whrrrrr, chip-chip-chip-chip...

*

Gasp. I wake up. I can smell him. I shoot out of bed. It's all right, there are the coloured women. Now the colours of red scarves, pink skirts, purple hats, green shoes whisper around my home. I'll follow them. I tread through endless landings, halls, searching. Always on the tail of a fleeting colour. Go up to the attic. There is a woman in green looking out of the skylight. She smiles.

–The stars are beautiful against the night sky.

I go beside her on tiptoe.

–Yes. I breathe in. *And you can smell the night.*

–*It washes your skin.*
–*Bathes your hair.*
–*Holds your face.*
–Quiet words.

The stars watch us watching them. Four eyes peeping at a multitude.

*

Tonight, as soon as my eyes open, I know they won't close again. Not without vivid images of red blobs and smiley teeth, warty noses whizzing around in front of me, branded on the soft, pink tissue of my inner eyelids. So I stay up. I love being able to do this. This was one of the things I'd wanted to do when I was younger. Freely, when I wanted to, at ten past two or something in the morning.

I go back down to my room, but instead of going downstairs for a drink straight away, I stand in the middle of my bedroom and look around, allow the milky darkness to drift on my skin; goose pimples its kiss traces. Go to the window and look out. Look down first, at the dark grass. Green lost in nighttime.

Everything different in this time. The rhododendron bushes are perfectly still, noiseless, yet speak endlessly into the night garden. At sunrise, they censor their voice and masquerade with light tunes singing through their scent. But these masquerades are real enough. Just another side. Their night voice is heavy and can crush if you are not strong enough.

My eyes lift past the bushes, over the wall, into the endless country beyond, then up, up, up into the night sky, searching slowly for a creamy moon which reminds me how small I...*we* really are.

I would love to see the flight of an owl across the moon, a silhouette cutting a hole into the perfect surface. I might try and see the town. It's special to look on a sleeping civilisation.

FIFTEEN

he Universal Mother also looks over the sleeping town. She never rests; she is always watchful. Her eyes follow and rest on her disciple worshippers. She holds each of them in her full womb, feeding them with her life's blood, her mother's milk. The body keeps them together: bound by one long umbilical cord, they are fed by the same nectar. The Mother's milk drives the body. It nourishes while they sleep, the flow tingling through every breast, every womb.

The women feel this flow and worship its course. They depend on the easy wisdom passed down from the Mother and drink of the same teat. A teat not offered to male lips. They do not have the breast or the womb for the yolk to feed into. The blood is cherished. The blood flow denied, unwanted. Keep the jet in the chasm. A sacred pellet from the Mother. A gift not to be sold through the body.

SIXTEEN

'm going to have a baby, you know." The red woman stretched lazily on her bed. She didn't care who she spoke to. The white woman still stood over her. Sara had come over and gone upstairs as the red woman shouted down to her.

The room held three women in its soft, blue sphere. A girl, red hair and knee socks, sat on the edge of the bed perusing a box of jewellery. A woman, stark and bright, stood at the bedside. Another woman, flushed and creased, lay on the bed. She sighed. "I'm going to have a baby, you know."

The stark woman continued looking over at the sprawled figure; Sara continued her inspection of a collection of amber. Whether they listened or not was of little matter to the red woman. She continued to fire out random phrases as she lay looking up at the cool blue. The sentences shot the air with firm precision, not aiming for a bull's eye, the target was the whole space of the air.

It came to her that she needed to create a pathway. A route leading up her stairs so she could continue to plan her baby in the proper way. So the red woman collected her pink leaves and arranged them carefully in a haphazard manner on the stairs. She left enough space to walk up and downstairs without crushing the crisp shapes. An orange lamp at the stop of the staircase emphasised the veins in the painted pink leaves, so the red woman could remember the flow of life pulsing through her when she became pregnant. In the gaps between the leaves, the woman placed books open at particular pages, the smooth, clean white of the paper and the warm print of the words a neat sight.

Sara had left a couple of hours earlier, as the red woman had seemed to forget she was there, and it was getting late. She closed the door quietly behind her, pausing for a moment as she thought she heard another woman's voice, then shook her head and walked home beneath the lamplights.

Back in the house, there was enough room for a considerable number of books, and the red woman passed luxurious time choosing the right ones. She needed something else—something to be dotted along the banister railing—but always something beautiful. The woman looked closely at the splay of colours in her lounge; she reached out and touched the different blobs, feeling the warmth on her fingertips. She was amazed.

"You know, darling," she inclined her head slightly towards her white figure, "you know, there is more love and beauty in this one room, with just the two of us, than there ever was before."

She stroked a circle of yellow cast on the arm of her chair.

"Yes, all along, from the start, I knew I wouldn't be happy there. Because, darling, I wasn't loved. Not really loved. He didn't understand anything real. Ha. I don't think he understood me." She patted the yellow circle, and it jumped from the arm of the chair to the top of her hand. She could see her blue veins snaking through the yellow.

"Of course, I loved him. Well, that is, I think I did. These things aren't as clear later on in life, are they? Still, I wasn't a child when I married him. But I didn't know it would be such a drudge. Being a housewife. For that's what I was, darling. Can you imagine that? Me, a housewife! I remember the day we moved in. We both stood gaping, and then he put his arm around me and told me we would be so content and not to worry, he would sort out all the money, I could stop at home and enjoy the house and garden. Pah. When I think of that, it makes me wither.

"Anyway, I didn't enjoy the house and garden. Well, it was just so boring. He thought we should agree on the décor, but I thought, well, if I'm the one in it all day every day, then I should be the one to decorate. We didn't argue about it, darling." The woman looked at the white figure. "I wouldn't let him. I wasn't going to argue about anything so ridiculous. And I told him so, and he laughed and held my face in his hands. He had beautiful eyes too, darling, but not pale like yours.

"We decided to spend the rest of the evening in the garden, it was such a beautiful night. We took out two chairs and sat holding hands. He said he felt he could burst. I said I'm not so bad, I didn't eat as much as you. I never was a mind-reading type, but I did get the feeling he was talking about something else..." She trailed off while her eyes drifted across the wall to a sliding square of orange. She watched as it stretched into a rectangle and then bent thinner and longer and then slowly twanged back into a square. "It took me a while to get back into shape afterwards. I suppose all the reading didn't help either. But we did love the world of reading, darling. I want colours and forms now. He was always talking about that little book of fairy tales. It was a beautiful little rectangle of dreams. He always called it *Flora's Fairy Tales*, but I can't remember the exact name. But I'm done with words now. Oh, well, it doesn't matter anymore." She laughed. "It didn't matter then, I suppose. Well, darling, where was I?"

Later, the red woman went into the town centre. She looked around the street, the people, as she moved from shop to shop. She noticed it was the time of day when oestrogen bubbles and seeps at the side of the road, a hot lava flow of hormone infecting the pavement.

Masquerades were unveiled as the physical absence of man seeped the town with the disciples of the Universal Mother. Some women exhibited signs of worship through their physical bodies as they waddled under bloated bellies. At the same time, they held hands with miniature tokens of their devotion to the goddess.

At this time of day, these bloated women declared the fertile state of their bodies upon the streets. The men are not privy to the amalgamated power of seeded wombs. Their penis withdraws and limpens, their body retreats and tires, and the women gather secret strength as they march, in formation, through the daytime streets.

The red woman saw all of this. She seemed to hover over it all like a distant voyeur. She was a heretic through her lack of adherence to the code. She didn't collect symbols of the sect to her hand and breast, child and suckling babe. She was as fascinated by these acts of worship as if a man herself. One difference: she was horrified by the ugliness of this monotony, this repetition, this lack of innovation.

SEVENTEEN

LOOK OUT THERE...GAZE *into the near and the far... it will guide you...these glistening drops and ephemeral streaks of windblown sun hover around my window like fairies...dazzling and fleeting, they are almost incapturable...almost...*

*

My dad's legacy of this *oh, magnificent!* house works with the secrets of outside. I have the room to sit and listen, to sit and watch. And yet listen: these fairies live everywhere, not just on the moor. They are the tiny, bright capsules of water flung from the clouds onto tentative fingertips, onto...they invite our senses to read their story but are happy to exist, nonetheless. I know this. I have learnt it myself by watching and listening.

The cellarman has taught me about the castle, though. He says it is something that lies along the path, not at the end of it. The cellarman says it is something to look forward to because it is a place of endless adventure and solace. My father also hinted at the castle but in different words, and he has given me a real castle here, in which to practise.

If only he had left some of the keys or the codes to navigate this house. It's somehow different from when I was little. It's grown! There are places I never knew existed, passages that snake away to unknown rooms, staircases that spiral to other worlds. It's kind of...alive.

I hope we grow together.

EIGHTEEN

he red woman had been sitting up for hours. She and Sara had been playing with the Barbie dolls the girl had brought over. After a while, Sara had to go. "It's my bedtime," she explained. The red woman nodded but didn't understand. She was engrossed in beautifying the cold, stiff women.

"Okay, darling. Thank you for coming." She didn't look up but carried on threading a blue ribbon through the synthetic blonde hair.

Sara started to pick up her dolls. "I can bring them over again if you like."

"Yes darling." Brushing hair, threading ribbons. "Wait, what?" The red woman looked up and stared in baffled fury. "What do you mean, 'bring them again'? They must stop here. I haven't finished."

"Oh."

"You don't have to take them, do you?"

"Well, I don't have to, I suppose. But that's what you usually do."

"I usually do? I do nothing of the sort, dear. What are you talking about?"

"I mean, they're my dolls, so I take them back to my home."

"Well, erm..." The red woman had taken up her doll again and carefully brushed her hair. "Well, how about they stay over here for a while?"

"Like a pyjama party?"

"Party? Yes, a party! A beautiful party. Beautiful...okay, darling?" From her position on the floor, the woman looked up at the young girl.

"Okay, I'll collect them in a few days then." Sara headed for the door.

"Yes, dear...mmm...okay." Absentmindedly, she stroked the hair with her wrinkling fingers.

Halfway through the night, the red woman placed the finishing touch on the last doll. "There." She leant back and admired her work. She had woven ribbons through some of the dolls' hair—through plaits and pigtails and buns. On one doll, an enormous amber-and-silver brooch was pinned; painted faces smiled back at the woman reclined on the carpet. For the moment, she was content to look at her creations, but then she counted them—fifteen altogether. Not enough. Where could she get more? She would buy some of her own. Her very own.

She went out and into the town. It was pitch-black, not a person in sight. "Oh." She walked down the street, looking around, and paused at one shop window when she saw a display of dolls in pink cardboard boxes. "Yes, those are exactly right."

She tried the door, but it was locked. She thought for a moment and then tapped on the glass. She waited for someone to answer. No one. "Maybe they're busy," she mused. She turned away and walked back to her house. Damn it. She wanted those dolls. Still, she would prepare everything just right while she waited to be able to get them.

After a night of thinking and appreciating, resulting in an exhausted nap, the sun came slowly through the curtains, casting a weak, green light over the room until the red woman sat straight up. Right! She should be able to get the dolls now; surely the shops would be open.

She strode slowly, looking all around her as she went. Early morning workers, full-to-the-brim buses, dog walkers, pushchairs crammed with babies and toys on coils. She'd never felt so inspired in her life—this was everything she wasn't! And yet it was feeding her with some sort of muse! She knew she'd done the right thing to wither away from her previous life.

She came to the shop with the display of dolls, and after pausing to feast her eyes on the wide variety, the woman stepped into the shop. She wandered until she reached the aisle packed full of little plastic women. She picked another fifteen dolls off the shelf and then, after a thought, another one, and carried her basket to a till.

"Started early for Christmas?" The woman at the till bleeped the boxes across her scanner.

"No, my dear."

"Oh. Well, there's a lucky girl out there for sure. Is it her birthday?"

"Whose birthday? It's nobody's birthday as far as I know. These dolls are for me, my darling." The red woman frowned, then smiled at the curly-haired shop assistant. "They're so beautiful, aren't they?"

"Well, yes. The girls usually like them."

The woman skipped home with her dolls, emptied them onto the floor and carefully removed the packaging. She collected the pink card and piled it up on one side. She lined up the Barbie dolls and began to titivate them as she had the previous fifteen. When the dolls were complete, the red woman slathered superglue over their backs and artistically arranged them over her bedroom wall. The dolls with special attention paid to their backs were stuck face-on to the wall, so a full tress of hair could be seen. They were not left rigid but were allocated movement in their arm and leg joints—the red woman was very considerate about that—so they did not look like sacrifices but self-made offerings; the arms reaching out, the legs lifted in joyous dance.

Wonderful!

It was time. There was no need to wait any longer. The time was right, her artistry ripe. Also, she was desperate for fresh canvas. Either that or she would have to go into town, and she couldn't bear the smell of oestrogen any longer.

Yes, she would go out and clamp herself onto the necessary paintbrush. She downed some wine then sifted through her wardrobe. She wanted to wear something vibrant, to liven up the dull colours of outside. Red was the most appropriate colour, but she didn't have a dress the right shade. Still, the cut of some of these was perfect. What the hell.

She went downstairs to her store cupboard of paint and carried a tin of bright red back to her bedroom. Taking the dress with the most-favoured cut from the wardrobe—a nightdress—the red woman laid it flat on the floor and smeared the paint on with her fingers. She became so absorbed in this ritual of smearing and drying, three days and nights passed without sleep, food or movement.

On the fourth day, when the painted dress was completely dry, red and stiffened, the woman stripped naked and applied make-up and perfume to her body. She twittered and laughed as she thought about the maturation of a living sculpture inside her body. She was almost jealous of the walls of her uterus, which would be watching her work grow while she was waiting and unable. Never mind. She could do something her womb couldn't. She would perhaps read to it, from important books of beauty and music.

The apprenticeship thus begun, she would educate her daughter about the importance of beauty. She could buy an overhead projector and cast artistic images onto her belly. She applied a fourth layer of lipstick as she looked down at her body. She had stepped into the stiff dress and stroked the hard paint resting on her hips.

"Perfect," she told her reflection. She drifted downstairs, past the glowing woman who had resumed her place in the lounge, and out of the door. She felt exhilarated and yet, as always, composed.

Her feet crunched over the driveway gravel, a sound holding an affinity with the cool bite of the night air. Her bare shoulders didn't feel the cruel whip of the breeze but received the kisses from a thousand glittering mouths. She reached a bar and ordered a drink.

She took it to a table in front of the open fire and watched the light from the flames play with the red liquid inside the glass. She put it to her lips and felt the flames curling down her throat, the colours washing through her and painting her inside as she had painted her outside. Yes, this warm dark red was just the hue she needed for tonight.

NINETEEN

Mrs. M, Mrs. F and Mrs. D were all sitting at home, in their lounges, passing the time with their uterine wisdom. So absorbed were they in the gems of their wombs, none of the three chatted to their children nor took up a book.

Mrs. M, Mrs. F and Mrs. D all sat slowly sipping tea. They spent every afternoon and every evening in this way, absorbed in their work, polishing their sagacity. This intellect was so innate, so deeply established, Mrs. M, Mrs. F and Mrs. D didn't need to concentrate on the process of their genius. They merely watched sporadic flies of thought pass before them. And remained unamazed.

TWENTY

She didn't notice him come in, sit down and take up a paper. She was fixated by the wash of colours coming off the fire. They bathed her skin in a sore pink, flamed her dress more potent. She became alive as she sat by the fire. The flames overtook her and made her part of it, so the open fire grew and grew as the woman's body became it. She sat there flaming and licking, her skin hot and changing. She could feel the white woman's energy burning from her!

The paper man took a deep draught of his drink. His gaze rested on the flaming woman. Her black hair, lifted by the intense heat, slithered around her shoulders like twisted snakes, licking her eyes and mouth. She was drinking and looking at her pinkened arms. He folded up his paper, went to the bar and bought them both a drink.

"For you." He put the drinks down and stood in front of her.

"Hmm?" The pink glow seemed to deepen.

"A drink. I've bought you one. You looked lonely, I thought."

She gazed up at him in surprise. "Lonely? My darling, when one speaks of being lonely, it shows a sorry, ugly self."

She turned and watched the fire before turning back to see the glow of the flames on his smooth jaw. "On the contrary, I am feeling most sociable."

"Good. I certainly didn't mean to suggest ugliness. That wasn't my intention at all."

She looked at his earnest face. He was beautiful. And his eyes were full of life spark. "You know about beauty?" She accepted the glass of wine. He could be perfect; his sperm would be perfect; sweet-smelling, quick. Her fingers twitched to mould her child of beauty.

"What is your room like?" She leaned towards him. "You are in a room, aren't you?"

"Yes, I'm here for the night. It's very good. Clean and tidy. Fine for me."

"No, no, what colours, what shapes? How do the walls look?"

His face held a shadow for a moment, as if he was uncertain of something he could see. Then he quickly shook it away. "Why don't you come and look for yourself? I'm sure together, we could...pretty it up."

*

She carefully took off her dress, laying the stiff garment on the floor. "Don't tread on it, dear. It might break."

She encased him strongly, a snake eating and digesting its food, only now, no outline of the meal was evident, the figure of the female body too sturdy to allow its shape to be transformed by the prey. She planted herself around him, sucking the core into her so life could flourish and then, once the nectar was taken, the root could be discarded.

The woman lay back, smiling as she thought of her baby starting its journey of beauty. She lay lost in her connection with her budding apprentice. She didn't hear the incoherent ramblings of the man beside her. She dreamt of colours and envied the privileged eyes of the child.

But wait. This hotel room was no place to build her daughter. She leapt up and put on her dress. She needed to be at home, in her art, the dolls watching, willing the burgeoning of a new beauty. Excited about her latest artistic triumph, the red woman didn't cast a backward glance at the man now asleep on the bed, but she did notice the thankful absence of an ugly snore as she skipped out of the building.

When she arrived home, she ran into the lounge and straight up to the banshee. Her white woman startled as she cried, "I did it!" then ran upstairs, through her tunnel of veiny leaves and clean words and into the bedroom. She twirled around, reaching for the dolls with outstretched, flickering fingers, then flopped onto the bed singing.

*

The glow in the corner of the lounge intensified; a smouldering ignited to a flare and then back to a white smoulder. *She's up to something. She's...she's changing.* The white woman flickered. *There's another life in here, something budding...I can feel it.* She stretched out her long, white fingers, turned her hands over and looked at her palms before bringing them back down to her sides. *How can there be room for three of us? Could I...could I ever be a mother?*

TWENTY-ONE

I am stuffed full of those remnants of feelings which stem from others and are fed by ourselves. I struggle to see the castle along the way of the path, and yet I can see it all the time. Printed on my eyelids, on the notepad of my soul. It is too distant now to view from an easy perch. I'm so restless. I can feel it constantly and can't reach it.

The castle stands alone yet jostles for room along with the other elusive creatures...that book...the fish...why do some crop up again and again while others only tease me? Their presence seems so urgent. And then gone but not quite, it stays with me and I am left trying to grasp the intangible, invisible object, room, person.

I spend time sitting at my library desk, thinking. I need to clear me some breathing space. The foreign bodies of unwanted memories dirty my waking life, so I struggle to find a space to live. That's when I go to my library and, for a moment, stand in the middle of the room.

I look around at the shelves of different worlds. I take down a thick book and feel settled by the familiar weight. I turn it over in my hands, allowing the weight to distribute across my palms, pressing on every crease in my skin. Then I thumb through the pages quickly, again and again, remembering the story planted on the white sheets, the massive world in these thin wisps. I sit, having started to read the first page. This is medicine and music and balm all in one for me.

Later, my mind is softened by other stories and words, and strangers' faces have faded...they become less real... I can cope with their existence...I have grown again.

I decide to go for a walk and drown any remains in the marshlands and peat bogs. It is grey outside, and wild, but the burnt oranges and browns lift the flat screen of the sky. The wind is lovely. The raw tingle in my nose is a symbol of union with the elements.

I march through the garden, keeping pace with the fallen leaves, through the gate and onto the moor. I keep my steps fast to make up for my morning of weakness and to jolt my body into action. My dad used to walk like this, marching quickly and steadily, never out of breath, always feeding off it, always taking note of the different lives he was passing through, walking along with. I can feel him with me now. We're walking in step together, and at last I can keep up.

I take a right turn to walk to the next house, and here Dad leaves me. He'll meet me later after he's looked at the lake. I walk up the hill and rest at the summit, observing the old, grey building. No one lives here anymore, hasn't done for a while, but I can see an orange light from a tiny square window and fancy it is cast from a desk lamp. Yes. It is the writer writing her book, wrapped up on her own in her awesome grey house with one light, a pen and a watching girl for company. And she must feel me, because I am willing her to, just as I am willing to know what words she's putting down, right now, as I stand outside so, when another girl in another library takes down a book to lose herself in another world, there will be a small fragment of a girl standing alone in the outdoors with the smell of cold air and orange leaves on her clothes.

I stand washed in this for a long time—so long that when I come back to the moor from the library where a girl is reading a book with my shadow in it, all is covered in dark. The sky threatens rain. I come back with a gasp. It had been so warm in the other place; I hadn't felt the wind smacking my bare face till it was raw.

I wait to adjust to this temporal change and stand with my arms outstretched so the wind can flap through my open coat and lick my body. I tilt my head back and close my eyes, feel the rush of blood and gale, then open my eyes up to the livid sky. My face is charged by the energy in this rolling darkness. I am privileged to be here at this moment and no longer envy the writer sitting with her lamp, writing down what I am in, painting the sky with her pen, while the sky paints my body with its own hand.

TWENTY-TWO

Dorothy Perkins. Mrs. M, Mrs. F and Mrs. D twitter their way around the racks of sequins, chiffon and starched, black trousers. Women saunter about with glassy eyes and handbags or pushchairs. Ragged husbands are dotted about like hatstands, weighed down with offloaded shopping bags, coats, umbrellas. Their appearance of acquiescence makes it difficult to decipher their feelings on being rendered a clothes horse. Their blankness is uninterrupted by filial demands. They are allowed the luxury of setting off their minds to heights of...

"Oo, love, these trousers are perfect for you, aren't they? Don't you think?" Mrs. F turned to Mrs. M as she held a hanger against Mrs. D's hips.

"Oh, I don't know. Those kids have ruined her stomach." Mrs. M turned away to look at some beige jackets. "This would cover it up nicely, love."

"Oh, but she has such beautiful legs, though. Takes after her mother there, don't you, love? Doesn't she?" Mrs. F nodded as she sorted through the rails waiting for Mrs. M's affirmation.

"You're right there, love. Yes, I say you're right there. Lovely legs—thank her mother. She gave you a gift there, eh? Oh, yes."

Mrs. D looked pleased with herself and surreptitiously glided over to some clothes near a long mirror. She fingered a red, strapless top while she glanced sideways at her mother's legs in the glass.

"Honestly, you don't half know how to get under a woman's feet." Mrs. F poked her rooted husband to get to the changing room. "I say, don't they get under your feet?"

Mrs. M followed her into the changing rooms shaking her head. "Oh, I know, love, I know. Mine's under them night and day, and that's not even starting on the kids. Sometimes I think we were sent even to guide them from the dinner table to the television."

"Oh, yes, I know what you mean. Ha."

They tried on garment after garment, barely looking at their changing reflections. Outside the dressing rooms, glassy-eyed men stood dotted about, never stooping, never weakening.

PROPHECY

TWENTY-THREE

never looked back, darling. Never. Not while I was walking down the gravel path or anything. Why should I? I was positively stagnating, dear. Who wants to look back on a quagmire of rot? I had nothing beautiful. No one appreciated the art within me. If only they had let it surface. But no, darling, it had to be a solitary thing. A woman cannot have a man and be beautiful. Or do anything beautiful. They are so bloody demanding, it drains the juices."

The red woman lay listening to her growing egg. She was still flat on her bed, giving her unborn plenty of space to spread out. "I need to change this outfit," she continued. "This isn't right anymore. But I can wait, just for a while longer." She nodded to the dolls, who held out their plastic arms in an embrace. "Yes, I know, dears, but in a little while. Shush now, I'm listening." A bright figure stood in the doorway. The red woman shaded her eyes from the glare. "What? Darling, what on earth have you done to yourself? No wonder you're crying, dear. I would be. Just look at the colour of you—you're positively stark. Is it permanent?"

No answer.

"Well, you'll have to try to wash it out yourself, darling. Whatever have you used? I didn't know I had anything so glaringly white. Anyway, I'm busy right now. Making a baby, you know. I'm concentrating very carefully."

The white woman moved closer to the pregnant body. A halo seemed to have formed around her whole figure. Each flicker of bright light produced a quiet wail. She went and stood over the red woman and looked down into her face.

"What are you doing? I told you, darling, you'll have to try and wash it out yourself." The red woman closed her eyes to the crying light. The white woman lurched forward to embrace the woman on the bed.

TWENTY-FOUR

y moonlight ramble through my home is one of my favourite things in the world. I'm always looking, always searching, dreaming of a discovery. It is never the same through the house. It changes constantly, independent of my own touch. Things come and go, pass; some stay; everything is stamped by a whisper. Tonight is no different.

After my walk out on the moors, I'd gone to bed with a hot water bottle and snuggled my quilt under my chin. I didn't sleep but lay like this for a while listening to the fading cries of the birds, watching the room darken, and with the dark, the books and paintings assume a different kind of light. The light that comes with the dark.

They lift out of their positions on the shelves, the walls, the floor. I watch the new colours and pictures growing, swelling with life. I can barely take my eyes off their beauty, mesmerised by a process which, although I can see it happening, I can't quite believe.

Every night I feel this bulging phase of life. I feel it when I am creeping through the hallways, when I am watching the gardens through the window—I can feel it even now as the sound of crying scatters the house with sharp confetti. A cry which flows as steadily as coloured shapes of tissue tossed onto the air. The pink and yellow and blue tissue shapes slice through the entire house and fall, not silently but with the tinkle of splintering glass. I get up to see where this is coming from, and as I move, I sense the pulse of living objects bulking out the air.

When daylight comes, they will soften back to their more passive form, but in this time, they are swollen, and I push through to seek out the musical wailing. I step onto the landing outside my door and feel a shower of silver water perfuming the deep oak panelling. I hold out my fingers to let the tinkling colours kiss my skin. I walk across the landing and up the flights of stairs; the crying gets louder.

I pause as I reach the attic and watch the chiffon scarves lifting gently in the breeze. The colours are brighter tonight. As they lift and flap, I can see a white figure sitting with its back to me. The stark glow reflects onto the scarves and infuses them with light. I move closer to the figure and see that the weeping comes from her.

Walking around the front of her, I kneel and look up into her face. Her eyes, although red and swollen from constant crying, are extraordinarily beautiful. "Oh." I clasp my hands over the white ones in her lap. "Don't cry. Please don't cry. Everything's all right." She looks up. I kiss her forehead. "Don't cry. I'm here."

TWENTY-FIVE

he red woman lay still on her bed. She was wracked with a great tiredness and an urge to sleep. But if she slept, she would miss the breathing of her art and the effect of the turning colour on her belly. Sara had called to see her, but the woman had neither the desire nor the energy to play dolls. And besides, she was not about to destroy her female wall art. She told Sara she was busy.

"Doing what?"

"Art."

"Art? But you're just lying down."

"I know. You obviously can't appreciate it, and I'd thank you to leave me now, as I have a terrible headache."

Sara had gone, and the woman had not moved. Her head ached; her body felt drained. She could not get up.

After four or so days, she thought it was time for the next stage. She went downstairs and was distracted by her face in the mirror as she passed through the hall. "Oh, darling, you're terribly pale." Her reflection stared back, wasted, gaunt. "Yet somehow…rather beautiful."

She passed her hand over her forehead and held her head back. Her sunken eyes almost disappeared in a pocket of greyish purple. "I must go and sit down." But for the moment, she was enchanted by the purple around her eyes and the thin delicacy of the skin. She was entranced by how this looked against the hard, smooth black of her pupils. She held her face close to the mirror and gazed at the colours on her face. The elegance of these contrasting hues was emphasised by the haggard appearance of her face.

Although her body felt like it was dying, the red woman was captivated by her own beauty and luxuriated in her own ornamentalism. She changed into a long, white dress and held her stomach. "My body is your canvas for the moment. Then it can be Mummy's turn." She looked again in the mirror. "This almost reminds me of someone...I don't know. I don't think anyone's been here."

She twirled a feather boa around her neck and shoulders and sighed. Her head ached terribly, and there was a deep gnawing in her stomach. She had locked her front door and refused to answer the doorbell or the telephone. "Can one never have any peace? Just when it is so important."

She slumped on the stairs, comforted by the pink glow of her leaves. Stroking a clean, white page, she rearranged herself into a pose more appropriate for a dying swan. She was so tired. Her body craved nourishment, so she fed it with words and images and tenderly caressed the purple smudges under her eyes and the black shadows widening across her cheekbones.

*

The phone had been ringing for hours, days, decades, an infinite shock of offensive round spirals looped around the red woman. The darkening woman. At one point, she had tried to answer it, but her body was poisoned with lethargy and allowed her to travel only as far as the wine cupboard. She carried it back to her place on the stairs and pressed it to her belly. The deep red against white cloth...

In the beginning were thoughts; now, there was colour, movement. Even her stillness was art. Her final stillness in particular, she thought, was pure aestheticism. And this time, it was for its own sake, as no eyes watched the performance.

*

The red woman lay on the stairs, in the passage between her lounge and her bedroom. In the middle. At the end.

TWENTY-SIX

I sit with the white woman in the attic. The low sunlight fills the room as I point out the various spots of delight, but only the chatter of birds on the slates responds. The white woman is...I don't know. Composed? Tranquil? Certainly soothing. I feel the compulsion to talk to her. The soft light blankets us both enough to keep us warm but not so much as to smother our quiet bodies. It yields to our breath, permits the birdsong to pass easily around it, whispers a tranquil word. And from underneath this garden of yellow-orange light and soft wood, I hear an old, old sound.

I rise to answer the doorbell, down, down, down the staircases, open the front door, such a marvellous piece of craftwork.

"Hello?"

"Miss Flora Morrigan?"

I nod.

"We're terribly sorry to inform you of some bad news."

Nod again.

"Your mother passed away last night."

TWENTY-SEVEN

I t was a still day. The sun fought to break through the mid-morning mist. A sudden flight of crows dropped a scattering of cries through the thin sunlight and shattered the stillness. Across the road over the church wall, a small procession was entering the heavy, studded doors.

The toll of ten o'clock brought Mrs. M, Mrs. F and Mrs. D into a small circle. Their greeting this morning was flavoured with an acrid excitement as they hovered near the church wall. Their eyes flitted from one another to the church, to surrounding townspeople, back to one another. Their eyes spoke faster than their tongues could curl around the words. A coffin emerged from the church, and Mrs. M, Mrs. F and Mrs. D slowly unfolded from their circle to form a line opposite the graveyard. They tut-tutted as the procession came into view.

"Well, well, fancy that," Mrs. M said.

"Yes, I know, lay dead for three days," Mrs. F said.

"Really? I heard five," said Mrs. D.

"Well, whatever," said Mrs. M, "that's one odd 'un out of the way. I mean, fancy somebody living like that."

"Oh, I know, yes. Never mingling. Never socialising in the community."

"Always keeping her curtains closed. Well, I mean—how can anybody be expected to know if there's something wrong?"

"Yes, hmm, doesn't do any harm to be a little more open."

"Oh, yes. Yes, definitely."

They watched the coffin as it was lowered into the ground. The small gathering around the grave listened quietly to the priest's final words.

"Well, well, well," said Mrs. M.

"What is it?"

Mrs. M gathered her bosom knowingly.

"Well, well, well, who would have thought it? I'd almost forgotten about her. Ha. And I'm pretty sure her own mother had. Forgetting her own daughter. Tut. A disgrace. Well, at least she's shown up for her mother's last do."

"Tut, tut. Yes, fancy her showing her face."

"Haven't seen her for years—nearly wouldn't have recognised her myself."

"Well." Mrs. F congregated her fellow sisters close to her lips. "Talking of children, do you know what I heard? I heard she had another one on the way." She nodded and pursed and stepped back to admire the effect of her revelation.

"No! At her age? Well..."

"Well, well..."

"Yes. Our Sara told me. Now then."

They frowned at the procession in disapproval.

"Well, I would call her passing a blessing then. And a double one for that matter. What child would want a mother like that?"

Mrs. F and Mrs. D shook their heads.

"Puh, and the Good Mother only knows what the child would have turned out like."

Mrs. F and Mrs. D nodded their heads and pursed their lips.

The town hall clock tolled eleven times. The women looked at one another.

"Shall we?" asked Mrs. F.

The women walked across the road to the café nodding their heads.

TWENTY-EIGHT

A strip of bright autumn blue and a stripe of white cloud marked the sky during the funeral. The bare tangle of branches spread flat against this brightness, the web of black stark and dazzling.

Now the blue strip has dissolved, and the sky has softened into a whole grey-white of early evening. The light from the sky drops, and the dark in the garden lifts. The flat black loses its stark quality, and a wash of grey seeps over the porous trunks, branches and bushes and plumps out the foliage. It is not dark, but that searching grey light, which becomes so padded with the imminent night, it is difficult to see.

It smells cooler, more damp. The wind is beginning to speak in its own tongue; there is a taste of bright winter in the air. The feel of change.

Things come...and pass. They are all part of a greater journey.

Beyond the house, above the moors, past the clouds, my mother and her celestial-born child soar freely. Their release unlocks something further, and I breathe deeply as I turn to go back into the house, which is bustling with life and colour. A rainbow is more beautiful than just one shade.

I smile. There is another figure living in there now. She will soon come to know herself. I won't force her. We'll both have much to busy ourselves with, weaving our own fabric of reality.

And now, it's time for me to start writing that book.

The End

Flora's Fairy Tales

For you, Mum.

AT THE CORE

here once lived a woman deep in the heart of the planet. Turn left at the atmosphere, down past the thin blue line, right on to the leafy tops, down through the tree roots, straight ahead at the crust, continue until the core turns liquid, then navigate through to the inner solid.

This woman listened to the creakings of the world.

The whispers of the trees told her of the animals who sought shelter in their branches. The raindrops brought her stories of all the strange encounters they witnessed in the sky. The tectonic plates grumbled about the footsteps of humans, and the core revealed secrets tucked deep inside the magnetic field.

The woman listened to all this and wondered, what was the use in listening if she could give nothing back? When could she take a turn in this conversation?

"You have no need to do anything," Core assured her. "You are right where you belong, here."

"But I want to make a difference," she lamented. "And besides, nobody knows I'm here."

"We know. But see how the world above reaches down to you as much as they reach up."

The woman was silent. There was no point arguing with Core.

She shuffled and shifted about, listening to the changes up above until she could bear it no longer. She wasn't going to argue, she wasn't going to justify. She was just going to go. Billions of years of pressure pressed on her. Earlier on, it had been mere curiosity, communication, but as the millennia went by, a different feeling caused a deeper sense of pressure to go. Duty. Responsibility. Care. She wondered how she could get up there. She'd never left the heart before. She seemed to have always been here. Would she survive up there? She took her bedroll and worked her way up through the layers of heat, molten rock, sediment, crevices, roots, landfill shit, pipe work, up, up, and up, and out. Out into grey light.

Grey light?

This is the light the surface lives work with?

No.

All was not natural up here anymore. They were more in the dark than she had ever been. She caressed the nearest tree, patting the moist bark. The dog that had recently pissed on it trotted by, tail in the air, nose to the ground. He was right to make his mark. He signed his name to his shit.

The humans walking about looked pale and had strange electromagnetic fields around them caused by the plethora of devices she quickly picked up on. Some had no core field left. There were plenty with a core spark still, which was a relief. She understood now the whispers reaching down to her and the magnetic field secrets. They were the ones reaching down to her.

Core was right. Her work was being done from within.

She travelled back down to the light from where she had come.

And she knew she belonged in just the right place.

Listening more carefully than ever, she set to work with the knowing of the vastness of love she held greater than duty or responsibility or care.

TREE WOMAN

he woman coughed and coughed. She looked out of the window onto her small garden outside as she rubbed at her old chest.

The mountains, the woods, the rivers lay behind the modest colours of her garden. It had been a long time since she'd travelled to them. The cough returned, and she scratched her gnarled fingers at her skin, longing to dislodge the seed that was growing there.

The seed that had been sown on the day of her husband's death. Her life's mate. Her love gone; her chest blocked.

People still came to her for healing. They travelled far from over the other side of the mountain. They came with sodden legs where they had traversed the river.

Others came scratching their heads and slapping their arms, from fighting through the depth of the woods.

They came and took what healing they could from her, straining with impatient ears over the rattling interruption of the cough. It was cold still, but there were signs of spring in the garden and a vibrant flush of green on the mountains.

The old woman stoked her fire and scattered some pine needles on the flames. The smell put her in mind of the last time she'd run, naked, through the forest, her darling husband chasing her and laughing.

They loved the air on their skin. It nourished them. Watching the flames flicker, she saw the pink cheeks of a young girl who had visited her some weeks ago. A beautiful girl, with the natural spirit of a True One.

She'd come seeking validation of Self. The old woman coughed, feeling the seed broaden in her chest, her tubes tight and painful.

"My dear," she said, holding a small hand mirror up to the rosy face. "All the validation you seek is here."

After the girl was finished, she turned to the old woman. "I'm so grateful for your time, old woman, especially with that dreadful cough. Forgive my impertinence, but you need to release that when the time is right."

The girl was wise.

It was, of course, the old woman's choice. She had to look at what it truly was. To grow.

The time was now right. The seeing of the young girl was the sign she had been waiting for, unaware she had been waiting for it.

Spring was coming, the seeds were germinating. She left the cottage and walked. Through the garden, across the meadow, through the stream, into the forest.

Weeks later, the countryside was in bloom. The young girl carried a basket of early flowers she'd picked as a thank-you gift for the old woman.

She stopped full as she met a wholly new kind of tree in the forest. She dropped to her knees.

A seed bloomed from her blocked chest, surging forward from her mouth in a beautiful curve of branches and buds.

Old Woman, strong, sturdy, flourishing.

Birds nestled in her white hair, and bees and butterflies danced between her outstretched fingertips as the branches of her Self burst forwards with radiant, expanding life.

The girl heard a whisper, followed by a giggle. She looked around and saw a squirrel peeping at her from in the branches of Old Woman and knew they were both nourishing their naked bodies once again.

THE BOY WITH THE STICKS

here was once a boy who lived in a small cottage by the woods. At the edge of the woods, a wonderful river stretched out and spanned the world from tip to tip.

The boy left his cottage and came out of the woods to be with the river every day. He listened to the many voices in the ripples and stills, saw the faces, the torments, the joys, the challenges of the world.

He returned in the late afternoon to his cottage by the woods, to watch the sky set ablaze, to watch the snow fall silently down, to watch the birds retire to their nests. To watch the timelessness of time passing.

And it was quiet. Oh, it was so deliciously quiet in his cottage by the woods.

Yet each morning, he was compelled to go to the river to listen and watch.

He was a clever boy, and his mother had done much to teach him about the world he could feel before she left to do work at the other side of the woods.

He knew he could do something with these pictures and sounds he received on the river. He knew he could help ease the torments, offer guidance for the challenges, celebrate the joys. He began to feel compelled to interact with that world he could feel and hear.

One bright, orange morning, he collected many sticks from many different trees. He sat with each one close to his heart, listening intently to the ancient whisper entwined deep in the fibres.

The trees whispered to him, and his body absorbed the information he was to send to the world. Each day, slowly, he released a stick onto the river and watched it until it disappeared from sight. And he felt whole as he reached out to the world he could feel and hear.

The boy did this each day, until the mornings turned from orange to a crisp, wispy blue.

His wholeness splintered in the frost, and he wondered where these fragments of trees went to, and he stayed and wondered until three days and two nights had passed. When he was passing into the third night, his body shivered and became fluid. His form trickled into water, and he flowed into the river.

He flowed over the shining brown and green rocks, he flowed next to the grasses, he flowed past the forest, he flowed beneath the sticks and the sky and the clouds.

He flowed to the other side of the forest and pooled himself into a lake at the shore of his mother, who shifted with joy at the expansion of her son.

There, he watched as the sticks lapped to the shore, waiting to be gathered with joy by those seeking the wisdom of the natural world.

FLORA'S FAIRY TALE

re you sure you want to do this?"

Flora studied The One in front of her. There was emotion there. Concern. But then, one would have to be dimensionless to have no concern when thinking about incarnating on the level three green-and-blue planet.

"I've had a wonderful time here. I am sure. You called me yourself."

"Indeed, I did. But it is never a command. You are a free energy. You can be in these realms as much as you like."

"Then why call me?"

The One smiled, and a strand of geometry unfurled to brush Flora with her energy.

"You have the power to integrate realms."

"Doesn't All?"

"Yes, indeed. But you have the capacity in one Earth lifetime."

The geometry sparkled, and a flush of Love ignited Flora's own patterns. Her caravan ignited around her, warmed and cosy. "My pleasure then! I'll see you when I get back."

"Indeed, you will. Always follow The Golden Ray within. I am there."

And so, once it was that Flora had roamed freely among the stars. And she had no mother and no father, for they were both in The All and The One. And she enjoyed her freedom.

She sped through the quantum universe in her caravan, creating patterns with the trail of lights her travel sparked.

Sometimes, but almost never, she peered through to see the millions and millions of mothers and fathers on the green-and-blue-and-white orb The One called Earth. There was something fascinating and yet unsatisfactory about them. It was fun to peep.

These mothers and fathers couldn't hear her or see her. And neither could some of the non-mothers and non-fathers. The children mostly could, until they were stopped. And the beasts and plants and stones of the orb always could.

Flora laughed, and her hair flew around her sparkling lips and cheeks as she steered her caravan over to The Strands.

The Strands all quivered at once, so happy to see Flora on her adventure. They twanged and quivered and shivered, flashes of colour dotting the space around them. The countless different hums resonated around her as she laughed and told them where she was going.

"To Earth? That one there? Goodness, are you ready? Are *they* ready?"

"Of course I am ready. And The One says I am."

"Well, of course you are. But you will still come and see us?"

"Yes! I still can, can't I?"

"We know it is harder to when you first go there as a body. But we go straight through and across, so we're still here and there."

"You're everywhere!"

"That's right!" They jostled and twanged, deep notes, high notes, emerald tones and blue quivers. A rainbow of strands.

Flora harnessed the reins of her caravan and whooped as she headed straight to the heart of The Strands. She rocked in wild plasma fire as she merged and travelled down, up and out all at the same time, collecting cellular matter.

Flora absorbed her twinkling, blinking caravan, and in a flash, her light vehicle bloomed, then diminished to a destiny.

So it was that Flora was born.

THE ONE PLACED
IN THE MIDDLE

ho do they think I am?

They think I'm naïve. Young. Gullible. Easily malleable. Manipulated like children's playdough, happy to be manipulated.

I'm not. My knot has become Not.

They don't know that. They don't know me.

They certainly don't know I speak with the sun. That I gather the rays and beam them back out. I respect solar power. I have had many conversations with it.

This they would never know.

They don't know I harness the wind. True—I used to be scared of strong winds, but now that knot is a Not too. That was way before I remembered I am a witch.

They don't know I can sense fear and know when it isn't mine. They don't know I no longer work to transmute or repel collective fear away. I saddle that bitch up and ride her like a dragon.

They think I'm still the child of the group, but a conveniently older version that can be primed, poked, prodded and ever so pleasantly pestered.

They could be careful. They should be careful.

But I don't play about. This shit is serious.

I can harness the wind to wreak havoc, to make myself massive.

I can.

I do Not.

I do harness wind power, though, and in cases like these, that power is vital.

What do they think I am?

A leaf fluttering on the breeze, blown this way and that, at the beck and call of an external force?

I *am* the force.

Who do they think I am?

A naïve kid, no mind, power or purpose of her own, crouching in a cubby hole for the time to come out and perform, reveal, listen, serve at will?

I *am* the will.

I serve nothing but my own will.

I grab ill wills of others by the neck, collect the soul of them and fuel my own.

They don't know any of this. They think they are the life sages, the mages, the ones who know all. I keep that useless knot in its own tight bundle. While their serpent writhes and twists in a self-consuming slick, my serpent is free to rise.

I keep that a secret.

That is so much wiser.

THE GIRL WITH
THE GOLDEN COMPUTER

any times ago, a girl was born from the heart of a star, before it became a star, and she grew so large she came to find a home on Earth.

Deep in the wilderness of the city she lived, gathering information and sorting out a database of all worlds of knowledge.

She went out into her wilderness each day and saw the numbers and codes, the letters and signals floating around the people she sat and watched.

It was so time-consuming! But she needed to collect and collate, and the patterns in her database were so pleasing that it was worth the time.

Sometimes, when she was relaxing, taking a break, the girl would sit back and look at her symbols drifting around her in a golden mist. They fluttered and flickered in slow motion like golden butterflies.

They were her constant companions.

And they were her. She could see that.

Then she would go back to her database.

Organic golden technology. This was something that came woven in and spun out from the body, waiting to be pulled back inside, very much like breath. But the other fascinating thing: lots of people didn't see it. They couldn't see the dials and levers and computations in front of their very selves—that *were* their very selves.

This was technology.

This was medicine.

This was the portal into the Great Records.

This was The Hidden.

All waiting to be unlocked.

THE GIFT

nce, a young woman tended to the garden outside her wood hut, and she tended to this with a hoop around her middle.

It was difficult to manage because the hoop didn't quite meet in the middle and so couldn't always stay up, and she had to tend to her soil and vegetables with one hand.

The hoop hadn't always been there. In the time when she didn't need to tend to vegetables, she'd had a simple cloak of shining bright. But over the years, it had grown dirty, pulled at and torn, and the time came when her mother and father needed her to cultivate the vegetables; she couldn't seem to find her cloak, so she quickly fashioned the hoop.

It was an old frame found in the garden shed by the wall. She could attach material to it so she had a cloak of a fashion around her shoulders, but she hadn't found anything fitting to clasp it so her hands could be free.

Every day she rose, dressed, ate with her mother and father, washed and then went to put on her cloak hoop and tend to the garden. Her mother and father offered tools to make her task easier, but she always said the same thing. "Thank you, Mother, thank you, Father, but I am quite all right. I will see you at dinnertime." Then out she would go, into the sun, the wind, the rain, the frost. Only when it was snow would she have a different day in with her mother, tending to the kitchen work.

In the evening, they would sit around the fire and listen to her father's stories.

It was a happy life. One full of contentment.

The broken hoop was the only effort she had to make. And an effort it was. It was an effort that grew larger by the season, and larger with each refusal to her parents' question every morning: "Penelope, would you like to use some different tools? It may make it easier."

She always refused, saying she was quite all right with the tools that were housed in the garden shed. One evening, after their meal, Penelope's father asked her, "Why do you never make use of any other tools? Why do you not let your mother make you a new cloak?"

Penelope looked long at her father, then her mother. "What are the tools you have?"

"We have tools that would enable you to work with one hand or to use your feet."

She nodded to show she'd understood. "And a cloak? You would make a new one, like the silver one I had when I was younger?"

Her mother shook her head. "Alas, I have no material at all like that. That was one of a kind. But I would make you a different one, still lovely, and warm for outside."

Penelope kissed her mother and father. "I am very tired. I'm going to go to bed now. Thank you, but I am happy

to manage without the other tools and to keep my hoop cloak."

The parents smiled at her as she went up the small wooden staircase to bed. They looked tired, too. She didn't want them putting energy into anything other than what they already did, and she knew it wouldn't help her.

The next morning, she looked out of her little casement before going downstairs. The garden was covered in morning rays of buttery sunlight, and the scent of pungent earth wafted up on the wind and curled inside her nostrils. There was the promise of something new in the air. She craned her neck as she heard a humming from down the lane. An old woman was shuffling along, her face hidden by swathes of scarves and tassels wound around her head, her little feet poking out, shuffle by shuffle, from beneath layers of skirts and aprons.

Penelope withdrew her head from the casement and shuttled downstairs, through the kitchen and out of the front door into the morning sunlight. She blinked as the rays danced little motes in front of her eyes, and she was momentarily blindsided.

Caught in the golden space, a honeyed space.

The humming cut through the mesmerism as it came nearer and louder, shaking her free from the web of sunlight. "Wait!" she called over the garden wall as the little old woman shuffled past, humming. "Wait!"

The moving body of shawls, scarves and skirts halted. The humming, however, rang through the morning air like a spell.

Her breath drew in and out in rags, the rush and pause working her body. The humming wound around Penelope, but this web didn't capture her like before. This played the keys in her mind and woke something in her head she had forgotten she'd remembered. She stood for a long time, seeing, feeling, remembering, bathing in the hypnotic and fascinating realm that unfurled itself around and inside her.

The body of scarves and material ceased humming and turned to face Penelope. A set of crinkled eyes looked deep into the young girl, two bright-green jewels burning out from brown, wrinkled skin. "Good morning to you, my dear. Is there something I can do for you?"

Penelope stared at the sparkling, deep pools that threatened to pull her in. "I, I don't know. Perhaps."

"'Perhaps?'" A sound something like a juddering bark rattled through the swathes of cloth. "Then perhaps you should think before you stop an old woman on her path and cause her the painful job of turning around."

The old woman was still, and there was a busy vibration in the air. This stillness was not a pause, but a space. A space to fill with messages and reception and transmissions and visions.

A little bent finger hooked out from a long sleeve to form a crook. "You see, my dear, you do know why you called me back. So why do you not simply say?"

"I can't remember! It is something like a tune I have heard but don't know the name for. Or a song I remember yet I've never even heard. I can't quite grasp it."

The rest of the fingers unfurled from the sleeve, and the second gnarly hand reached out and clasped

Penelope's soft young hand. "Grasp this, my dear. You may not know the name for it because it has no name. Only essence. And when you know the essence over the name of something, then you have connected truly. Now, focus."

The girl in the garden focused. She felt gnarled and wrinkled fingers on her soft skin. She felt the gimlet gaze boring into her. She heard the swash of material flowing on the wind, flapping around them both, covering her in a cloak. For a moment, the sun disappeared behind a veil of silver. Stars shone. Silver light bathed them both and cloaked them from the world at the same time.

The essence was close now.

"Drink it, girl. Drink it in."

Penelope drank in the silver light. The sun came back out, and the cloak fluttered and flapped back around the hag, who turned and continued down the crooked path.

With a lingering look and the taste of starlight on her tongue, Penelope turned to start work in the garden. Free, she used both hands, knowing the essence was inside her, and she had toiled enough.

WITCH WIND
AND BARE BONE

he way to the witch wound through the valley. A pathway from the village eventually snaked into a valley of deep green and craggy rocks, ragged hills rising in the distance and framing the valley on either side.

The way to the witch was known through the tread of the worn path through the grass.

There was a change in atmosphere, as though the wind here was charged with personality. It almost spoke out loud as the craggy valley was entered.

The witch's cave was to be found near the top, well into the hills. I'd been to see the witch twice before, once to ask advice for an ailing relative, the second time to ask her visions on my future.

This time, I was going on a dare of will. I was seeking to satiate my enchantment with her.

Since my visits, I'd dreamed of her cave with its hanging feathers and sticks at the mouth of the entrance. I'd dreamed of her hair, tangled brown with glitters of silver shining through, and the deep, dark-grey eyes like shining globules of mercury fixed on me, unblinking.

I dreamed of her again and again.

Her words echoed around the cave of my memory in deep rasps.

How did she know what she knew? How did she see what she saw?

How I longed to see through her eyes, even if just for a fleeting moment.

I was climbing now to her cave to seek this.

The wind picked up as I left behind the village and the noises of men, the clatter of work. The wind whistled around like bellows, breathing bigger and deeper with each footstep I planted.

The breath of the wind filled me and touched me. It merged with my skin and drifted in and out of my body. I became the wind, and the wind became me. We remembered each other.

The rattle of bones stilled the wind, and I turned to face the sound. I'd walked past the cave! Hidden in plain sight, it had been.

Not now. The sticks rattled, and the witch stood, her eyes fixed on me, her palm displaying a clutch of small bones.

The silence roared.

Time disappeared.

I stood, in the blank, captive in her presence. Her voice, when she spoke, filled the vacuum like an unfurling of ocean, slow and distant at first, then speeding and crashing around me as her words broke in waves around my ears.

"You come wanting to see through my eyes."

Increasing circles of sound crashed around me, until they entered my skull and echoed around every inch of its chamber.

I had to summon all my strength to push my words through the echo chamber the witch had created. They could just manage to squeeze through.

They came out thin. "I feel compelled to ask you."

The witch looked long at me, her eyes scanning deep into my cells. Her voice, when she answered, was like the wind blowing holes through papery bark. "Then ask."

Now it was my turn to stare. I had no question. No words formulated into structure. Only sensation. Only compulsion. With a hint of recognition.

The witch beckoned and turned to go back into her cave. Just before she turned, she cast the bones at me. I caught them with one fist. I stared at the witch, but I could only see her long, dark hair and dress as she sank back into the darkness of her doorway.

I dared to look at the bones. They lay in my palm, one across two. The one was bare.

A bare bone.

Etched into the other two bones were marks, symbols, almost like letters in that I could read them, yet so unlike any letters I'd ever scribed back in the village.

Whichever way you turn, the path to follow lies always in front of you.

I was the bare bone.

The path was marked out.

I stepped up to the doorway. The witch was waiting as she faced inwards.

We entered side by side.

The earthy scent of herbs was both homely and strange, like a distant memory of a forgotten dream.

But there was no time to settle in. The witch opened the clutch of my hand, took the bones and thrust a hag stone at my face.

A swirl gripped and moved me, yet not a thing in the cave moved. I planted both feet as I was buffeted by the wind that came from nowhere.

The wind that came from somewhere.

The witch held the hag stone fast, and my sight was plunged through the hole in the flint.

A torrent of vision streamed into my senses. Faces loomed close, ugly and strange. Colours and lights travelled, a million messages encoded on each strand. My body rippled and pulsed with electrical overload, and I gasped to hold on to my breath.

"You see." The witch's voice cut through the sensory overload like a clean knife. "Now you see what it is to see."

I fought to stay planted on the ground, to manage the influx of faces, voices, information, sensations. Black roots grew down from my feet and spread deep and wide, anchoring me and keeping me from being buffeted by the blow of all of this.

The witch's voice trickled in again, now in the background. "Indeed. You do indeed See. Are you ready, though, Bare Bone?"

I rocked and rooted. My head was light. I battled to manage the influx and drew from within and without to stand in the storm of Sight. I could do this! I'd come here for this. I had to prove myself. My body expanded, and I felt like I was taking up all the space in the cave, in the town, in the universe. And at the same time, I was taking up no space.

I was ready, wasn't I?

The hag stone breathed, a rasping gasp that sucked me close to the faces and the codes, then sighed me out.

The whispers of the Other Worlds cloyed to my skin. My eyes were imprinted with a thousand visions.

The hag stone sat in my palm, innocent, unassuming. I traced my thumb around the smooth stone, describing the hole with respectful fingertips. I held it to my ear and heard the glistening tones of the universe. And woven through it, the whisper of the witch: "Etched on forever more, Bare Bone."

Startled, I jumped around for my wizened host.

The witch was gone.

THE CAVE

are Bone listened to the whispers that echoed around her cave and added her chants to the pattern. The darkness time had fallen, and this was the time for Bare Bone to look into the deepest shadows and etch herself. She had stories to tell, but they were not yet woven into the stories of her cave, not yet woven with the whispers she listened to.

She had closed off the cave so she couldn't see any passers-by. Even if they did know of the cave, she wasn't willing for anyone to enter her space. And so her cave was closed off with wards and allies, and all Bare Bone saw was the space of potential. The space of inevit ability. A space she was going to choose to enter. The darkness of deepest shadow and deepest time, at the end of which stood brightest light and highest space. Then the infinite loop of All.

This was her time. She was Bare Bone, and she loved it. The witch had marked her bare, had shown her the space, and she was not scared of stepping a foot into the abyss. She needed no one else's mark to write her story. She created her own. And in the moment of now, all was true.

Although she was Bare Bone, she was far from blank. She held the slate of infinite wisdom. And though the hands of many Others were in it, it was her hand in it now, that was all.

THE FORBIDDEN FOREST

I t's always forbidden, isn't it?

The forest full of fae, wicked witches, big bad wolves. The place where never-before-met men find and rescue you. Of course it's forbidden. It's riddled with lies and paradoxes.

And you just might figure them out.

The old woman in the depths of the forest—she wants to consume you, right? Wrong. She wants to savour your innocence at the same time as showing you crucial lessons, so you don't need a never-before-met man to rescue you.

I know. I went there. There is no wicked witch or big bad wolf. Well, there is, but not quite the one you know from the cautionary tales. Forget the cautionary tales of others—though they may have had their reasons for this—and enter your own story. The real fairy tale. Find your own big bad wolf.

That's precisely what I did that early summer morning, while there was still a whisper of nighttime in the early morning breeze.

I walked into the forbidden forest with my heart beating fast. I knew already this was a quest, and like every true quester, I would have to rely on my own resources. The first encounter was with the forest itself. The trees stretched over and around me, dark, leafy, almost silent. Imposing in their numbers.

I pushed through the silence to listen deep. They were guardians. Protectors. And hard workers.

The feeling settled, and that was the moment. I knew I was safe in this forest. And also at that moment, I had an inkling why it was forbidden.

Ancient truth.

Forgotten knowledge.

Forbidden wisdom.

I pushed on, willing to carry on the quest. A twig snapped in the silence, and I froze. A chatter of gnats clouded my vision, and I swatted them away before I realised they were not gnats at all but forest fae. I was getting deeper.

"I'm sorry," I said to the mist of fae. "I couldn't see properly." I'd caught myself in time. Admitting I'd thought they were gnats would have been a dangerous insult, a bullet I wouldn't have been able to dodge.

They clouded around my head still, challenging me to turn back, to close my eyes, to be repelled. I was entering into their domain, and that was risky. Forbidden?

I asked them pure and simple. "May I come in? I will tread lightly."

The tinkling sound glittered around my head, and they scattered to let me pass. I knew I would have to tread lightly. The passing through the fae mist was serious. The trees now were dank, black, and the forest was tightly bound. The chattering of a single magpie split the atmosphere.

But it was not back-to-reality that filtered through the split. The cry was the key to the Other realms.

Clutching hold of this knowledge, I forged through the binding branches, noticing the multitude of life squashed between and below them. Dank fungi bloomed in the nooks between branches and the carpets of mulched leaves and mosses. This was their home. They knew how to not only survive but how to flourish here. They had found their place.

I was searching for mine.

I stepped forward. I had hold of the keys.

The wet, black trees stretched on like time's unfurling tendrils. They stretched on and out and down and up until they became part of me. Until I became part of them.

As I unfurled myself through the forest alongside, upside and downside my companions, I saw motion in all its forms and guises. The sudden clearing that pooled in front jolted me into the Next Realm.

The Realm of No Time and All Time.

Standing at the boundary of the Next Realm stood a wolf. The big bad wolf of the forest. The big bad wolf of the fairy tales. Fortunately, I like fairy tales and live for stories, and so my eyes are used to coming face-to-face with them. My mind has travelled into them thousands of times.

My body hasn't.

My body met the wolf with the shiver of new adventure, the knowledge of one known but as yet unmet.

This wolf was not one to be feared, just respected. And met with a key to offer.

I had worked for my keys, and now I could show this key to unlock the way to the Next Realm. The liminal. The zero space. The All Space.

They tell you stories of big bad wolves as a caution, for this space in the forest is not for the faint-hearted. The clearing is only found through working the depths of the forest.

I stepped forward. I had hold of the keys.

The wolf turned and entered the realm by my side. The clearing was shrouded in a mist, a haze of darkness that seemed to rise from the ground. I was curious, not afraid like the stories had said the character would be. I had my key and my wolf.

I stepped into the dark mist that gathered around the ground and felt a rush of warmth. I felt Her arms around me before I saw Her. She pulled me close, and it was then I Knew.

There is a reason we have been warned.

Have the courage to find the real reason.

The End

ABOUT THE AUTHOR

Diane King is from Buxton, a spa town in the English Peak District, where she has found many characters and stories on its hillsides, up its trees and in its strange pools. She hopes you love reading those stories as much as she loves writing them.

To find out more about Diane's stories, visit:
https://www.diane-king.com

BEATEN TRACK PUBLISHING

For more titles from Beaten Track Publishing,
please visit our website:

https://www.beatentrackpublishing.com

Thanks for reading!

Printed in Great Britain
by Amazon